now playing

now playing

STORIES

SHELLIE ZACHARIA

keyhole press

Keyhole Press
an imprint of Dzanc Books
www.keyholepress.com

Portions of this book originally appeared in *Backwards City Review, Beloit Fiction Journal, Canteen, Coal City Review, Coe Review, Dogzplot, elimae, Emrys, Gander Press Review, Hobart, Juked, Keyhole Magazine, Mochila Review, Monkeybicycle, Opium, The Pedestal, Pequin, The Pinch, Potomac Review, SLAB, SmokeLong Quarterly, Steam Ticket, Storyglossia, Swivel, Ward 6,* and *Washington Square.*

Cover design by Peter Cole. Cover photo by Jonathan Bergy. Tyepsetting by David McNamara.

ISBN: 0982151241
ISBN-13: 9780982151242

www.nowplayingstories.com

For Roy

Uno!

Wednesday nights there's a group of us and we all meet at Celia's house and she makes us dinner and we get wasted and play Uno. She likes to cook for friends, she says. We're not about to question or complain because we get one night a week where we don't have to dig in our own fridges and worry about if the coleslaw is funny tasting or just gone bad, and we don't have to order take out from Mercy's Tavern yet another night, especially since they fired the one cook who used to throw in free bleu cheese dip with the sweet potato fries. We just have to bring wine or beer and head over to Celia's and she's making enchiladas or baked ziti or lasagna. One time Celia made jambalaya, which didn't go over well because she made it too salty, and we drank all the beer so early in the evening that Amy said she'd go buy more, but she got in a fender bender and called to tell us the bottles were all broken in her car and she'd see us next week. And Celia doesn't make chicken stir fry anymore because Robbie had an appendicitis attack that night which he falsely diagnosed as food poisoning until the emergency room doctor said, "Oh boy, that thing needs to come out," and so even though it wasn't food poisoning, Robbie associates stir fry with pain. One night Celia makes red beans and sweet potato curry soup, and she also puts some real good dope in the brownies and she tells us this when we get there so that we eat dessert first. And while we're playing Uno on the living room floor and we're calling out "Draw Four!" and "Skip!" and "Reverse!" and we're slapping down cards and thinking we're a pretty funny bunch of people and good looking too, then one of us, Theo with the goatee and sunglasses at night, says, "Isn't it great that this game brings us together in a circle, like we're all one here, you know, even though the name of the game is about another type of oneness?" Then he holds up his last card and shouts, "Uno!" before he tosses down a red four, and we all let out a collective "Argh!" and we just say, "Yeah, man," because Theo's a poet and sometimes he says what we've been thinking. He just says it better.

Why This Isn't a Good Story to Tell

See, you ask me what's going on, and I know you mean, tell me something good, but not much is going on. No stories to tell. Not one you'd want to hear, unless you count what happened two days ago and that's not really a story.

It's just about this old woman at the grocery store and how she couldn't reach the peanut butter because it was stocked on the top shelf. So while I was standing there picking out strawberry jam, I said, "Let me help you," and I asked her, "What kind do you want?" and she said, "Peter Pan, smooth, please." After I handed her the peanut butter, she said, "You're a little pretty and very nice." Then she said, "Hold on," and she reached for her purse, this beat up white leather bag sitting in the shopping cart. She took out her wallet and her hands were shaking and I said, "Oh no," thinking she was going to offer me money, but instead she handed me a business card and said, "This is my grandson. He's a nice boy. You should call him; he's lonely."

I looked and saw he had a nice boy name and he was a travel agent and he had a work phone and a cell phone and I said, "Thanks," and put the business card in my own purse, which was just a little straw bag because it's summertime. And since I'd had it with mean boys, it seemed a good thing to do, to call a nice boy, and after two glasses of wine that evening, I called the old woman's grandson. When I said who I was and how I got his number, he was quiet. I felt stupid, but then I felt even worse because he finally said, "I'm sorry. My grandmother isn't always well. I'm married. She forgets." Then he laughed and said, "Or maybe she does remember and doesn't like Jill anymore," and I heard him say, "Ouch!" like his wife Jill must have smacked him on the back of the head.

I apologized and hung up and drank another glass of wine because he did sound like a nice boy. And I went to bed and it was another night like so many of my nights.

So you see, it's not really a good story, not the kind you want to hear. No romance or adventure or mystery.

The guy didn't call back and say, "Forget about Jill, let's meet for dinner."

He didn't call back and say, "Actually, I'm from another galaxy and I want to create a new type of being with you. I promise you'll really enjoy it."

He didn't call back and say that he would love to make something happen between us, but he was very busy because he was a rock star, a spy, a pirate, or a guy about to go on a cross country journey to find out some great truth.

He was just a nice guy and he was married and he even thanked me for helping his grandmother.

He didn't call back.

End of story.

Lizzie Sharpe's Nose

The kids in Mrs. Ortega's fifth grade class are making figurative language foldables when Lizzie Sharpe opens a pair of scissors in front of her face and announces, "I'm going to cut off my nose."

And she does.

"Lizzie cut off her nose! Lizzie cut off her nose!" Albert Rubio stands up and yells. Mrs. Ortega is about to shout at Albert, well, because she's always shouting at Albert, because Albert is always yelling out or hitting someone or tapping his pencil on the desk, but then she sees that Lizzie has her hands cupped to her face. Lizzie begins shrieking and Albert pulls at his spiky hair and hollers, "Look, look, it's right there!"

Mrs. Ortega rushes over and says, "C'mon, Lizzie." She dashes to the classroom sink, grabs paper towels, tells Lizzie to hold them on her nose, and then she ushers Lizzie by the elbow to the front office.

"Lizzie has cut off her nose," Mrs. Ortega says loudly as she bursts through the door, and the secretary, Virginia Martin, who has seen and heard countless stories, raises her eyebrows, says, "Have a seat," and looks up Lizzie's mother's phone number.

"It's okay, it's okay," Mrs. Ortega says, her arm around Lizzie, but she thinks this is not okay, no way, nothing like this has ever happened in her classroom in her twenty years of teaching. Never. There was Piper Ramsey who sat on a nail a couple years back, and Charlie Keagan fell off the monkey bars at recess and broke his arm, and this year Richard Sanchez threw up on Haley Crane's shoes, but never, never, did anyone cut off their nose.

The principal, Mr. Brock, comes over and says, "Let's see, Lizzie," and Mrs. Ortega takes a look also, and the tip is gone, sure enough, it isn't there.

"I've got to get back to my room," Mrs. Ortega says.

"Can you bring back the tip, please?" Mr. Brock asks, and Mrs. Ortega thinks, absolutely not, oh my, okay, yes I will.

Mrs. Ortega finds twenty-five students huddled on one side of the classroom, all except Albert, who is inching his way forward in exaggerated pantomime of creeping.

"It's on her desk! It's on Lizzie's desk!" Haley Crane says.

"I saw the whole thing!" Albert says, coming up to Mrs. Ortega.

"Tell me what happened, Albert."

Albert fixes his blue wire-rimmed glasses on his face. "Well, Lizzie took her scissors and opened them up and put them around her nose. Then she said, 'Look, I'm going to cut off my nose.' And she did!" Albert raises his hands in the air. "I can't believe it."

"Well," Mrs. Ortega says, and that's all she can say right now. She snatches a plastic bag from her closet, a paper towel, and hurries to Lizzie's desk. Yes, right there, a small tip of flesh, the end of Lizzie's little bubble nose, sitting on a piece of green construction paper, obliterating the second letter *i* in simile. With her paper towel, she picks up the tip, drops it in the baggie.

"Everyone have a seat. I'll be back." She pops her head in Miss Hunter's room next door, says, "Miss Hunter, would you keep an eye on my class for a minute?" and heads back to the front office.

"Where is she?" she asks Virginia Martin.

"Clinic. Her mother is coming to take her to the emergency room."

"Don't smile."

"I'm just thinking Eddie Meyers will be happy."

And yes, Eddie Meyers, a third-grader, is somewhere in the school right now, and when he hears what happened, how Lizzie Sharpe cut off her nose, he probably will smile. Somebody else will now be the talk of the school. Just last week, Eddie wedged his head between the rungs of a wooden chair during art class and couldn't pull it back out. The school custodian sawed the chair and only then did Eddie's head come free.

Yes, Eddie Meyers will smile.

Lizzie Sharpe is not that sharp! Lizzie Sharpe nose how to cut things—get it—knows/nose. Homophones, homonyms? Hmmm. Who remembers? That Lizzie Sharpe, she's on the cutting edge of things—idiomatic, see. Or just idiotic?

When Mrs. Ortega calls her husband after dropping the kids at PE, she says, "Oh, Felix, this has been the worst day of my life," and she begins to cry. He says, "What? What? Is it Thomas? Is it the dog?" The dog is sixteen and blind, and Thomas is a teenager, but Mrs. Ortega answers, "No, no, no. Lizzie Sharpe cut off her nose in class today." And of course Mr. Ortega says—sooner or later someone would—"To spite her face?" and he laughs but Mrs. Ortega doesn't.

Back in her classroom, the chairs are in disarray, construction paper and scissors and glue bottles scattered on desktops and fallen on the carpet. Foldables are in various degrees of finish. Metaphor, simile, personification, words dropped on the floor, examples written in good and bad penmanship: *her eyes sparkled like diamonds; her cheeks were red as cherries; the toaster flamed like a dragon; the clouds shouted for us to get home.* The room smells of oranges and blueberries and black licorice from the scented markers the children like to use.

Mrs. Ortega sits at her desk. She puts her head down in her arms, closes her eyes. *Nobody knows/nose what a child will do.* There's her own son, Thomas, seventeen, who perhaps wasn't even in school right now. He'd become so rebellious. She should call his school, ask to speak to him, tell him about Lizzie Sharpe. She isn't sure how he'd respond. She knows that at one time, when Thomas was a young boy, he would have stared with open mouth, fork of mashed potatoes caught in the air, the family sharing stories at the dinner table. But now, well now Thomas wasn't home for dinner all that often—soccer practice, study sessions, meals at his girlfriend's house—and if he was, well, he might not even find the story interesting, not like Albert Rubio, who will tell the story to anyone and everyone tonight. Albert will tell the bus driver, his brothers, his grandmother, his father and mother, he'll tell them all the story of Lizzie Sharpe, and he'll use his fingers like a scissors, make the snip sound, maybe remember it's onomatopoeia from another day's lesson. He'll tell everyone he was the witness; he'll pull off his glasses in excitement and say that the class wasn't given homework this evening. This, Mrs. Ortega believes, will happen. But then again, she lifts her head and looks at the school clock, what will happen she does not, she cannot, really know.

Now Playing

First, let me say this: I do not hate Jonathan Green anymore.

Not in the least bit. Really. I'm over him and I'm over hating. I mean, he can't help it that he was, and maybe still is, a weirdo collector of wine bottles and women. Or that he's crazy. These things probably help his performances, which he says are biographically fictitious.

So I'm not holding the past against him when I write the review of *Green Chronicles: Disco Time at the Electric Quilt Factory*, his new play. Avant-garde theater experience, performance art, whatever he bills it as. That would be petty. Even though the last time I saw him was when we went to Thanksgiving dinner at his parents' house, then he dumped me in an unceremonious phone call a few days later. I should have noticed something was up, but I was overwhelmed by the Green family. Odd people. Oh, his parents tried to be nice—"Hello, so you're Jonathan's new sweetheart?"—but I noticed that word *new* and I saw the looks they gave me, eyebrows raised, the way his mother said "vay-gan" like it was some disease. And there was the tossing-of-the-cranberry-sauce-at-the-wall incident when his mother just heaved the dish. *Splat. Crack.* It was cool, but a bit dramatic. I see where Jonathan gets his artistic temperament.Seriously. There was no need for that at all. A little friendly banter about tough turkey and the task of carving, and the father went and got the drill from the garage. That was pretty funny. But then there was the cranberry sauce, like a Rorschach test on the wall, and Jonathan's sister Roxanne calling out, "Spaceship, monkeyhead, space monkey, iris in bloom," and Jonathan just sat there and drank another glass of wine and fiddled with the pilgrim maiden salt shaker. It was all nuts, if you ask me. I'm vee-gan, so I don't know what the turkey was like. Maybe it was tough.

Not that I can mention any of this in my review of *Disco Time at the Electric Quilt Factory,* because my journalistic integrity would be questioned. Usually I review movies for the *Chicago High Note*, a free local entertainment weekly distributed to all the hipster bars and coffee shops. I don't review new films. I do a column about good movies to rent, and I try to look back at the old fun stuff, because I feel like people are just so damn creepy and sad and weird lately. Like recently, I reviewed *Ferris Bueller's Day Off*, a classic feel-good movie with Ben Stein as the teacher calling attendance and repeating "Bueller, Bueller" in a monotone, and Matthew Broderick so young and cute. I smile every time. But the guy who usually reviews plays—or, in this case, "the theater of the absurdly real"—he sort of went nuts and moved to Alaska, because he wanted to learn about sled dogs and do the Iditarod. When he announced it, I said, "Holy shit!" and someone else said, "Hot dog!" and someone else said, "Cold dogs, if you ask me!" and everyone laughed, because we were drinking beers.

At the next staff meeting, when they asked who'd take over theater reviews, I said I would, because I'm looking to diversify. I don't plan to write for the *High Note* forever, although it's a decent job and not much hassle. Not much money either, but that's fine because I live simply. Which may also be why Jonathan dumped me. He couldn't get over the fact that I just didn't care about owning things like a car and a cell phone. Once, after he got upset when I showed up for a lunch date with my skirt slightly ripped by my bicycle chain, I said, "You used to find me charming." And get this, he said, "True," and that was that. Another time, he said he liked me because I didn't have an artistic temperament. It sounded like an insult, especially when I remembered how we had bumped into his old girlfriend, who was wearing knee-high black boots and a black beret, and after we made small talk and kept walking, he said,

"She was very moody. Artistic temperament," but the way he said it, I know he meant, "I'd like to fuck her again."

After I volunteered to do theater reviews, Noah, the editor-in-chief, said to me, "Hey, let's do Jonathan Green's new performance. Folks like his stuff." I could have then said, "Well, he dumped me after an intense relationship, and I'm still slightly scarred." But I didn't. Partly because I like to think I'm past it. I've been taking this tai-chi class through community education, and it makes me feel peaceful and fluid and I think it's generally improving the quality of my life. Chloe, who writes a do-it-yourself crafts column that teaches you things like how to make napkin holders out of old cereal boxes, says if I really want to improve the quality of my life, I should take the kundalini yoga class, because it gets you in touch with your sexual energy. I'm thinking I may try it, though from Chloe's description of the people in the class, I'm not totally sure I want my sexual energy pouring out. Or theirs pouring in.

I guess I also didn't say "conflict of interest" to Noah because he's this great guy and I have a small crush on him, even though he's married to a girl I'd like to hate, but I can't. I still have high hopes anyway. Maybe one day, she'll look at Noah and say, "Honey, I love you, but I've got to go do the Iditarod and won't be back for like ten years, so I think it best we split up." Seems ridiculous, but not really, given that nobody ever thought Walt, the guy who did theater reviews, would move to Alaska, and he's there now, crying out *mush* and *gee* and *hah* and yukking it up with the Inuit. Things like that happen.

And really, I'll admit this, I was curious to see Jonathan.

While I'm admitting things, I should say I wasn't there for the beginning of the Jonathan Green performance, and maybe this hindered my understanding of just what the hell was going on. I have a reason. I was ready to leave my house with plenty of time to spare. I wanted a good seat close to the front, so I could let Jonathan see me seeing him, and I planned to be really pleasant and extra-smiley, so he'd know I've gotten over him, because I hate the idea that he thinks I'm lonely or miserable. Which I'm not. Most of the time.

But right before I was about to walk out the door, my neighbor Trudee came over. She wanted to complain about her husband, and right in the middle of a sentence about Asshole Javier (her name for him), she stopped and said, "We need to trim your bangs. They're way too long. It makes you look old." Old? Well, of course I had to let her trim my bangs. Trudee's in cosmetology school. She snipped and snipped and finally she said, "Looks good. Go get 'em, Tiger," because Trudee talks like that. Then she was gone. Leaving me with crooked little bangs, like a tiger had chewed my hair. There was no way I was going to the performance looking like a mauled freak. I had to use my kitchen scissors, and I cut and I cut again, and by the time I got them pretty straight, I hardly had any bangs left. I was younger-looking, for sure. Like about five years old. I have to say, I cursed a bit. OK, a lot.

I know I could have gone across the hall and asked Trudee to help before I hacked away. But I have this issue where I want people to like me, which may be why it bugs me so much that Jonathan's mother seemed to not like me and probably said so to Jonathan and maybe influenced his decision to break up with me. I mean, I wasn't the one who said the turkey was tough, and I wasn't the one who was drunk enough to laugh when the cranberry sauce hit the wall, and I wasn't the one who did this litany of weirdness about just what the sauce looked like. I was just a guest, and when all that happened, I sat there quietly and sort of smiled and poked around at the mashed potatoes, because there was no way I was going to explain to his mother that the butter and milk weren't good for me.

So by the time I got to the theater, I was fifteen minutes late. I have a feeling I missed the whole setup for why a woman was cutting up fabric and tossing the pieces all over the stage, and why a girl in mismatched knee-high socks was doing some line dance while a strobe light flashed and a ghostlike voice said, "This ain't your momma's disco," over and over again. I kept wondering if it would all be explained in the playbill. But I hadn't picked one up at the door because I was late, and because the ticket taker kept doing this weird chicken clucking thing with his tongue, and I took it as a reprimand and hightailed it past him without grabbing a playbill. I had to stop in the bathroom first, and no, my bangs had not grown on the way there. A woman was crying into the mirror, like she was watching herself cry, and I thought maybe she was an actress because she was just standing there staring at the tears on her face. So I got out of the bathroom pretty fast, and by the time I snuck into my seat in the last row, I felt pretty whirlwind.

I mean, "This ain't your momma's disco?" Hell no, it wasn't, and I knew Jonathan's performances were out there, but I couldn't help thinking that this might be beyond that. Close to bad. Maybe Jonathan had been struggling since our breakup, and maybe, just maybe, this play was proof of that. But I wanted to be impartial, not stoop to pettiness and write a bad review, and I wanted Noah to think I was quite fabulous, just in case his wife really did decide to do the Iditarod, or even just take off for her parents' home in Sweden, so I tried to have an open mind about what was going on at the front of the theater.

About thirty minutes into the performance, some disembodied voice announced that everyone should put on their 3-D glasses. Jonathan was on the stage, snipping scissors into the air and reciting from the "Lotus Eaters" section of *The Odyssey* and looking very handsome. I was really upset because I didn't get a pair of 3-D glasses *or* a playbill and I wanted to go out and yell at the chicken clucking guy, because I felt like I was missing the point of everything. Everyone was giggling and adjusting their glasses and staring at the blobs of color on the screen that were interspersed with real photographs—which I realized, after a few minutes, were pictures of Jonathan and his family. I kept thinking that there might be a picture of me, but there wasn't. While everyone was making noises like they were amused and awed, an older man in a business suit stood up in the third row and shouted, "This is the worst thing I have ever seen in my entire life!" Then he pushed his way past the people in his row and walked out. Everyone got quiet, and even Jonathan paused in his recitation, just a beat before he continued. I swear he said my name—Sarah—but then someone behind me laughed and said, "Que sera, sera." The man next to me, who had his 3-D glasses pushed up on top of his head, leaned in and said, "Was that part of the performance?" and that got me thinking that maybe it was. And maybe it wasn't. It made about as much sense as everything else that was happening, so I smiled and pulled at my bangs and asked if I could look at his playbill.

On page two, I found information that I hoped might have cleared some things up: *My mother was knocked down by lightning when she was 25. It didn't hit her, just near her. She was putting laundry on a clothesline. The shock made her hair stand on end. After that, she had an urge to quilt. She hasn't stopped since.*

Except that it didn't clear much up at all.

Nor did the folks wrapped in quilts who stood like mummies at the side of the stage.

Or Jonathan reading.

So much of it didn't make sense that I started focusing on the woman sitting in front of me. She had the most beautiful hair, long blond curls that corkscrewed perfectly and fell far down the back of the seat. She had this nervous habit of pushing her fingers into it, scrunching it, fluffing, and the handsome guy next to her seemed to really like her because he kept leaning over and whispering into her hair. Anyway, her hair was fascinating to me, more fascinating than anything going on in the performance. Two girls came out on stage and did a Greek choral thing—something about artistic vision, which also involved more 3-D viewing of pictures of people painting and reading. And again I thought maybe I'd be in there, one of those Saturday afternoon moments when I was flipping through a magazine while Jonathan stared at me and called me fabulous, but no, I wasn't part of the montage.

I don't know what got into me. I could say it was the wine, but I hadn't had any. I don't know, but at one point I reached out to just touch the woman's hair, one of the curls that hung longer than the others, and who would have thought she would have felt it, but she did. She turned around and glared at me through her 3-D glasses. Then she lowered them on her nose and damn it to hell, it was Jonathan's ex-girlfriend, the one he still wanted to fuck, the one who writes and directs movies and has an artistic temperament. I said, "Sorry, I dropped my 3-D glasses," then made this big pretense of looking for them. I hoped the guy sitting next to me hadn't noticed any of this. But of course he did. After Artistic Temperament turned back around, he leaned in and handed me his glasses and whispered into my hair, "She is beautiful, isn't she?" and after that I just got up and walked out and headed to Murphy's for a few drafts.

So I have no idea how Jonathan Green's *Disco Inferno at the Quilting Bee* started, and I have no idea how it ended. Really, I have no idea what happened in between. I suppose I should say I can't write the review, but most likely I will. I've got a job to keep. I'll use witty metaphors about the fabric of our days and piecing together memories. I'll use words like *electrifying* and *outrageous,* and I may even mention that it made people crazed with emotion. That they leapt from their seats. I wouldn't be lying, and right now that's good enough for me.

First Draft

1.

Roxanne quit her part-time job at the bakery, saying it was in the way. Who could write stories, expect to be called a writer, when there was chocolate to spread, cinnamon and nutmeg to sprinkle, pecans to chop—an endless movement of floured or sticky hands.

"I'm sorry, this is not working out," Roxanne said. She handed her apron to the owner and wondered if there was some personality test in how the smudges of ingredients worked themselves onto fabric.

Sitting at home, she did not write. Instead, she bought white Christmas lights, strung them in her kitchen and spent hours with ivy and rose stencils making one bathroom wall look like a quaint garden trellis. When Roxanne painted, she recited lines from *Romeo and Juliet*.

"Aren't you writing?" her best friend Carol asked.

"Who can compete with Shakespeare?" she answered.

Roxanne took to buying wind chimes and clay pots and glass paperweights. All this for ambiance, but still the storytelling was hard. She paged through writing guides she'd acquired as an English grad student, and said "*denouement*" in bad French, leaving her mouth open in exaggeration. She spoke English, some Spanish, but her French had always been poor. Even at the bakery, she had never faked it—she did not say the "*qwa*" in "qwa-sant" like the bakery owner did—who was in no way French, just a guy from Houston.

When she was awake, she struggled, thought, "Wasn't I once a genius?" And when she slept she wrote lines and lines, numerous first lines that all sounded promising. They could go somewhere.

"But where?" Roxanne asked as she sat up in bed, heard the ticking, flipping of the old clock radio's numbers. The cat, a Siamese who slept at her feet or sometimes curled against her stomach, did not answer. In fact, the cat—who was large—seemed to be getting larger. Roxanne wondered one evening, after a glass or two of chardonnay, if the cat was eating her words, digesting the lines of her story, inhaling plot.

"That is the roundest thing I've ever seen on feet," a guy she was dating said when the cat waddled by. She looked at the guy and thought unkind things, but said nothing. She was lonely.

This new boyfriend listened to her read her stories. He seemed distracted, though he nodded as if he were listening. Moose was a pilot, was there and then gone, which she didn't mind because she needed solitude.

"Don't you need money?" Moose asked.

"Yes, do you have any?"

He looked startled. She laughed. "I have come into money."

Moose said, "How much?" and she shook her head at him. She would not tell.

"Enjoy Portland," she said, opening the front door. "Bring me bags of peanuts."

One night, while reading a new story to Moose, Roxanne realized he was sleeping. His eyes were in that eerie half-opened position, so that she wondered if he would rise, a zombie ready to devour her. Perhaps she ought to try science fiction.

"Moose," she whispered. "Moose."

He didn't move, and she left him there, on what she had termed "the guest side of the bed," and got up to make a cup of tea. It was midnight; she called her brother, Jonathan.

"Moose is sleeping," she said. "Is that a bad sign? I put men to sleep after sex and my stories."

"His name is Moose. That's the bad sign," he said.

~

"How are you doing?" her graduate advisor asked. "Will you return next semester?" He called like this every few weeks. He had told her last time, his voice like maple syrup so that she wanted to marry him, "I don't want someone with your talent to quit the program."

Roxanne glanced at a piece of paper held between two fingers. She had bought an origami book. She made folds and reverses and edges and came up with tulips and elephants and roosters. She used pages from her stories to make the pieces, which she placed around the house.

"I'm building an origami garden," she finally said.

She liked the precision of origami. It was so different from trying to make something from nothing—stories from words, words from mind. "This morning it's a goldfish."

"You're a storyteller, Roxanne," the advisor said. "Don't give up."

She looked down at her fish. His fin was too long.

"You are getting too weird for me," Moose told her.

"Weird," she said. She did not say what she wanted to, that he was weird, wearing his pilot cap to bed and asking her to whisper "Jet man" in his ear.

He held up a piece of origami.

"That is a pecking crow," she said. "It is action origami."

"I think we shouldn't see each other," he said.

"See each other?" she asked, putting her hands over her eyes.

"Weird," he repeated.

"*Arrivederci*, pilot boy."

When he walked out the door, she threw the pecking crow and shouted, "Fly."

2.

"You need to talk to someone," Jonathan suggested. He was an artist in Chicago, performance art that involved bad Eighties music and people painted in day-glo. The piece Roxanne had seen last time she visited was about haircuts. By the end of the night, her brother and five audience members had shaved their heads completely.

"I'm talking to you," she said.

"Come visit. I'll let you read some of your work as part of my new scene on family. I'm using mom's quilts in it already."

"None of my stories are done. They're all drafts," she said.

"Maybe you should try poetry," he said.

"You're not funny." But when she hung up the phone, she wrote some lines, wondering about line breaks and syllable counts. She shouted "Free Verse!" like she was calling out a song request at a concert.

Sometimes life became a mishearing. As if someone called out, "Look at the moon!" and it was really, "Look at the bloom!" and you stare up at the sky even though it is midday.

"Witty, but off track," Carol said when Roxanne told her this. "Get busy. Don't piss your life away."

"Piss my life away?" Roxanne repeated. "What a rude thing to say in front of your baby." And she hung up the phone.

She called back in thirty seconds. "Just kidding," she said and hung up again. She waited for Carol to call back. Carol didn't, and Roxanne said to the cat, "If you piss your life away, just do it in the litter box."

One night Roxanne told the cat, who seemed to be ballooning beyond recognition, "Were I Scheherazade, I would be killed. The sultan would say, *Nice words, but I am bored. Tell me a damn good story.*"

The cat slept, so she called Carol and read her a story she believed was done.

There was a pause. She could hear the baby crying. "Is that it?" Carol asked.

Roxanne sighed, imagined she saw the sultan wink at the executioner, a slight movement of his arm.

"And then a lion jumped through the window."

3.

At the video store Roxanne found a Sundance movie whose writer and director and star was a girl she had gone to high school with.

"I can't believe it," she said aloud.

"It's a good one," a man standing near her said.

"She's a beautiful woman." He was with his son, a boy of four or five. Roxanne wanted to say, "Shut up," but instead she said, "Rent this one," and pointed to a video she knew was bad. "Loved it."

She read the back of the high school prodigy's film box: *"A delightful story of friends searching for meaning in their lives. Some choose to look to the past, others look to the future. They seek new homes, relationships, and families. A story that tries to answer, with humor and intelligence, what's missing?"*

"Oh god," Roxanne said aloud, putting the movie back on the shelf in the wrong place. "Of course that's the story. It's always the story."

She called her brother to tell him. "She's cool. We dated for awhile," he told her.

"When?"

"Couple years back. She lives here in Chicago."

Roxanne sighed. "You don't tell me things."

"You should rent it. Great film," Jonathan said. "She's pretty hot, too."

In the bookstore she noticed a woman slip a cookbook in her oversized purse. It made Roxanne nervous; she tried to avert her eyes before the woman noticed her noticing. She felt guilty, an accomplice, and when she passed by the cookbook section, felt her heart speed up when she saw the empty space, right there between *Cajun Cooking* and *Catfish and other Southern Meals.* She considered what was missing—possibilities—*Cakes for All Occasions; Calling all Cooks; Canned Vegetables—No Way! ; Capellini or Fettucini: Know the Difference.*

4.

After flipping through a literary journal that featured a series of nine photographs on consecutive pages, all the same photograph of a rose, Roxanne wrote a letter to the editor.

I am truly amazed by the photographs showcased in the last issue of your fabulous magazine. Recently I lost the negatives to my extensive photo collection in a house fire, but I did salvage some manuscripts. I am sending you one of my best.

Before she sent the letter, she looked at the magazine again. Yes, all the same photo as far as she could tell. "This is art?" she said aloud. "This?"

Then she called Carol. "We need to go self-esteem bowling."

"What?"

"Bumpers up. No gutters. We could be bowling queens."

"I'll get a sitter."

At the bowling alley, Roxanne announced, "We must wear funny socks with our bowling shoes."

"I don't have funny socks," Carol said.

"*Voila!*" Roxanne said as she pulled wadded pairs out of her purse. She had always wanted to shout the word *Voila*—say it correctly, though she wouldn't mind yelling out, "Viola!" just for fun. "For you," she said, handing Carol a pair of yellow socks with pumpkins. "For me." She put on a blue pair with teddy bears.

"Let's have fake names," Carol said when she sat down to type names into the electronic scoring screen.

"Self-esteem names," Roxanne said.

End scores: Glorious 115. Attagirl 84.

"You need practice, Attagirl," Roxanne said. She asked for two beers from the snack bar attendant.

"Winning ain't everything, Glorious."

"When I was ten," Roxanne said, "I was in a bowling league. Girl High Average two seasons in a row. Trophies for that. I'd win high score patches that I'd make my mom sew on my shirt."

"I played street hockey with my brothers," Carol said. "Got a black eye once."

"I was good," Roxanne continued. "Perhaps I peaked in junior league bowling. Maybe that was the great achievement of my life."

5.

Roxanne got a job in the bookstore, not in the café section, though this was where she thought she should work. She knew lattes and cappuccinos, appreciated the dark oiliness of espresso.

"But you know Chekov and Cheever," the manager said during the interview, which took place in the café and was poorly punctuated by the clatter of plates, the clink of mugs. The manager was pointing at the application, at the line that said Roxanne was a graduate student in English. It did not say she had told the advisor she must reevaluate life and needed a semester off. It did not say that Roxanne could not fathom finishing her thesis, could not hold a story together.

Roxanne stared at the manager. She wanted to say, "I'm not Scheherazade. I can't tell a story that will mesmerize. I will die when the sultan realizes this." Instead she said, "I know more than just the C authors."

While scanning the literature section, she found a pair of panties stuffed behind a collection of Poe. She thought she would never take her panties off for Poe, but maybe she would for Kerouac. She did not tell the manager, and did not touch the panties, but went home and added a thong scene to a story she was working on. Her character asked, "Where's the rest?" It was a bad joke, but she read the scene into her brother's answering machine.

It was the kind of response she had come to expect. Silence.

6.

Her favorite bookstore café worker was fired.

"I don't deal well with change," she told the new café worker, a girl named Melanie.

"Then put it in the tip jar," Melanie said.

Ha. Witty, young, I will hate her soon, Roxanne thought. "Cranberry scone, please."

On her break, she sat and ate, considering round table discussions as she stared up at the menu board. *If I were a sandwich, I'd be a* _______________. A good question for lively discussion.

Sloppy Joe, she decided, considering the weight and slide of her life.

~

One morning, while shelving books in the poetry section, she found a phone number neatly written on an index card and a photocopied booklet of poems, a coffee ring around its title. She stuck the index card in the booklet, hoping something wonderful would happen for someone.

7.

The graduate advisor told her, “Registration time is here.”

She sighed, trying to decide what to tell him.

“The computer suggested ‘fricassee’ for my misspelling of varicose.”

He laughed. “Use that.”

“I’m not even sure what fricassee means,” she said. “I’ll get back to you.”

“Come to town,” Jonathan said. “Come see the show.” Her brother’s newest show had just received good write-ups. “You’ve got time.”

Roxanne did have time. Her thesis, a slim collection of stories, was getting slimmer. “What’s the show about?” she asked, though she knew she most likely wouldn’t make the trip.

“Our homemade disco.”

“The disco!” Roxanne shouted. The homemade disco

had been in the foyer of their parents' home. They'd dress in mismatched clothing and turn the radio on loud and Roxanne would yell, "Flick the lights, flick the lights!" at the neighbor they invited over, a girl who never wore shoes. Then they'd dance, arms ricocheting and legs sliding along the linoleum floor.

"I loved the disco," Roxanne said.

"The story you read me was pretty good," Jonathan said.

Before leaving the bookstore one evening, Roxanne put one of her stories in the magazine section, near the arts and crafts magazines. She handwrote on the top of it in green pen, "What do you think of this?" She wanted a kind reader, and expected someone who made candles and dried flower arrangements to be kind.

Two days later she found the manuscript tucked behind a *Dog Fancy*—how interesting, the movement of objects—and scrawled in black pen, loopy script under her own green question, was a response: "Needs work. A little more of something."

On a day off, she broke down and rented the award-winning film by her high school classmate.

The film was good, sexy, she could not say it wasn't. "Shit," she said to the cat. She called Carol halfway through the movie and said into her answering machine, "I am just trying to find out what is missing. Don't give up on me." She paused. "Don't screen me either."

She wished she could hate the classmate. But this filmmaker had not been someone to hate. Just a regular girl. Not a cheerleader or a mean girl. Just a girl in Roxanne's English classes, where maybe Roxanne had been the girl to hate.

The end of the film was meadow and sky and clouds and then a spinning. There was the fluttering of a butterfly, yellow, and a woman giggling and then a fading of sound, a blurring of color into nothing. It left Roxanne slightly dizzy, almost breathless. She was not sure what the ending meant, but it was beautiful and that was something.

Stitch

In fourth grade, Ruthie Fowler got hit in the head with a baseball bat out on the PE field. Smack, just like that. She was too close to the batter, or maybe she was bent low, the crouching catcher. Poor Ruthie Fowler, who must have howled, and the players must have howled, and Brian Delaney, the batter, must have hung his head in shame and run off to hide under the banyan tree out in right field.

But I don't know. I wasn't there. I was inside my classroom, most likely figuring numbers, learning to memorize five times five, five times six, my voice with the others, little multiplying birds, peep, peep, twenty-five and thirty. And so I didn't know the score of the game and I didn't know Ruthie Fowler was rushed to the hospital or that Brian Delaney cried and Coach Wilson counted blessings and prayers.

The scar, of course, might not exist now. Just the ghost of a scar, like the ghost of a scar on my left foot from when I dropped the grape juice jar all those years ago, just a faint sliver, a white line, really not there at all. Her scar might be like that. Just memory and the tracing of a finger along invisible pain.

"This is the zigzag stitch," Ruth Glass says and points at the new sewing machine in front of me.

I am staring at the machine but what I really want to do is ask this Ruth, a Community Ed sewing class instructor, if she is Ruthie Fowler.

But I don't. I twist the dials and wonder why I chose sewing as my path for self-improvement. I lift and lower the presser foot. I try to make the machine pop and click while I watch Ruth walk around the classroom. She is short, round, her blonde hair cut in the fluff helmet of a woman who doesn't know any better. A woman who quilts and sews and paints watercolors on Sundays.

Zigzag stitch spidering above her left eyebrow could be hidden by makeup or time.

I am convinced.

Ruth Glass is Ruthie Fowler, moved to Texas after fourth grade, baseball bat head, Ruthie Fowler.

~

Ruthie Fowler was a big girl and her hair was cut with too straight bangs and her clothes were solemn and lumpish and she seemed an old lady to us in our cutoff shorts and sunburst t-shirts, fancy girls with pinks and purples and reds.

She was one of the girls in Art Club after school. She sat at the end of the long table in the art room, alone or with April Lapinski, who came to school sporadically because she had diabetes. I rarely spoke to Ruthie Fowler—maybe just things like "Hand me some green tissue paper" or "Pass the pipe cleaners." I did admire her artwork; it was lovely and pale compared to my own brash colors and imprecise lines. The art teacher showed me works by Matisse. She showed Ruthie a Degas book of prints.

"But I don't dance," Ruthie said when Miss Nancy showed her the book. "I'm fat."

Miss Nancy, with her paint splattered jeans and almost bare feet, sandaled and glittery-toed, looked at Ruthie and said, "Degas did more than ballerinas," and she flipped rapidly through the book pointing out, "See, see, see."

"Take out your patterns," Ruth says. She holds up the tissue paper, the lines and arrows an apron waiting to bloom.

Ruthie Fowler would want us to make aprons. Ruthie Fowler most likely made cookies and brownies. She made them with her grandmother and brought them to the church because that was the kind of girl Ruthie was—good and quiet and too old for fourth grade.

"Look for the fold lines," Ruth Glass says and I pull my pattern from its envelope. There is English and Spanish and size A and B and beige tissue paper spooling and crinkling in front of me.

Ruth holds up a pair of scissors. "Remember, never use your sewing scissors for anything else," she says and clips them, snip snip, in my direction.

I try to press out the tissue, but it is like clowns in cars, unmanageable and tumbling. The perfect girl sitting next to me with her blonde bob and pink nails smiles. Her pattern is laid out nicely in front of her. I don't smile back.

"Be neat," Ruth says and she is looking at me and I am thinking, you don't like me, do you, Ruthie?

The day Ruthie got hit with the baseball bat, everyone was talking about it on the bus ride home. Our words seemed to grow, their volume increasing with the afternoon heat and the wind whipping through the open school bus windows, until Mrs. Belafonte, the bus driver, pulled over to the side of the road. We shut up then.

Mrs. Belafonte heaved herself out of the driver seat and stood looking at us with her hands on her big hips. You could see sweat stains under her armpits when she raised her hands toward the rows of seats and said, "Let us pray to Jesus for little Ruthie."

There was some foot scuffling and uh-hums and maybe some other things before Mrs. Belafonte started out with "Dear Lord." I didn't hear much else because

I was Jewish. I had just started Hebrew School and so Mrs. Belafonte talking to Jesus about poor Ruthie Fowler made me feel weird. I scrunched down in my seat and looked to my friend Roxanne who sat next to me every day, and Roxanne was rolling her eyes and shaking her head, so I felt better.

And then Mrs. Belafonte's prayer was done and she plunked herself back down. She started the bus, and we were all pretty quiet the rest of the way, except Molly Spencer who kept muttering, "Poor Brian, poor Brian," because we all knew she had kissed Brian Delaney on a dare one Tuesday afternoon in one of the big tunnels on the playground.

"You'll need to backstitch," Ruth says, and she's standing over me and my pathetic floral monster, one pocket higher than the other, too thin, crisscross, mismatch-stitched apron.

I look up at her, look to her eyebrow, searching for the telltale line. She wears too much makeup, her pancake thick, her eyelashes like stitches themselves. "This looks like shit," I say.

"Yes, it does," she says.

She is definitely Ruthie Fowler.

Daredevils on the bus, a game that kept us busy throughout the school year, with Mrs. Belafonte sweating and praying and moaning in the driver seat, and us growing bigger and bolder with our dares as we counted the days until summer.

"Now don't hurt each other," she'd shout out and someone would shout back, "Never ever, Mrs. Elephante," and she'd smile into the mirror so we could all see her crooked front teeth.

I dare you to burp *I Love You Murphy Pennicamp.* I dare you to lick the back of the bus seat. I dare you to flick that redhead in the ear. I dare you to chew that piece of gum stuck under the seat. I dare you to eat a page of this math book. I dare you to touch Ruthie Fowler's stitches.

"You can do it," Roxanne told me. "Then tell me what it feels like. It looks puffy, doesn't it?"

"I can't," I said. "She's in the Art Club. She'll hate me."

"Just touch, Carol," Roxanne said. "You don't have to lick it."

It was quick. A fast tip of finger to the black stitches and I was back in my seat. Ruthie Fowler turned around to scowl at me, and Mrs. Belafonte looked into her bus driver mirror, her eyes narrowing, and then there was her great big voice, "Carol Kellerman, now you leave that girl alone!" I sank low into my seat and Roxanne, all giggle and knee pat, whispered, "What did it feel like?" I was silent all the way home with Roxy coaxing, "Like a bug? Like a centipede? Like a zipper? Like moss?"

After our fourth and final sewing class, we all wear our finished aprons and head to Bert's Tavern. We drink beers. Things get loose and people speak truths. Miss Pink Nails and Perfect Apron tells us about a vampire sex show she saw in Germany. Willa of the sunflower appliqués talks about Spanish fly and her boyfriend with the right hook penis, and Grumpy Mavis with the frizzled black hair and blue fish pattern tells me—with a heavy pat on the back—that my apron is by far the worst in the class. We clink beer bottles and talk about what other community courses for self-improvement we might take.

"Golf."

"Thai cooking."

"Ballet."

"I'm thinking watercolors," Willa says.

It is then that I turn to Ruth Glass and say, "Are you Ruthie Fowler?"

She blinks slow and says, "I am."

"I'm Carol Kellerman," I say. "We went to elementary school together."

"Carol Kellerman," she says.

"Starmount Elementary. In Miami."

"Yes," Ruthie says. She stares at me a moment then shakes her head.

I pause for what seems too long. She sips from her beer. "That was a long time ago," I finally say.

"Yes, it was," she says and smiles.

I look down at my lap. I pull at a loose thread on my apron pocket. When I look up, Ruthie is still staring at me. She rubs fingers across her forehead and takes another sip from her beer.

Nine Roses

Inventory

Like a centerpiece on the front lawn: a row of movie chairs, red velvet seats spotted with use, and around the chairs, pillowish piles of clothes, a haggard line of men's shoes, wingtips and loafers and a pair of hiking boots and one baseball cleat still dusted with orange clay. Stacks of novels, musty classics and newer paperbacks, mingle with moisture-rippled comic books, bundles of *Superman* and *Spiderman* sorted and rubberbanded into rolls. A wicker basket bursts with old tennis balls and a couple of rackets with strings sprung like uncooked spaghetti.

Sprawled upon an almost white sheet: decorative soaps in a cigar box, neckties, plumbing accessories, incense burners and packs of incense, a large wooden dolphin statue painted in rainbow colors, a gaggle of marionette puppets, jars of marbles and jars of nails and a jar of beer bottle caps and a shoe box filled with film canisters.

Propped against three pine trees: nine framed black and white photographs.

The small woman

She sits in her house, crying, her small hands twisting around an old baseball cleat in her lap. She is skinny, her hair cut short and boyish, but she wears a floral print dress. Her bare feet are pulled up under her, cross-legged. She sits in an old armchair and stares out the window at the front lawn and weeps.

The older woman

She is old, large, her faded red t-shirt tight across torpedo breasts. The t-shirt reads "Spike House Baseball Camp." She wears tight black pants, a pink scarf wrapped around her head gypsy-style; the pink of the scarf and the red of her shirt make her look like love, a Valentine, but the scowl on her face doesn't fit. She stands with her hands on her hips, her bare feet planted firmly in the grass. She guards the items strewn across the front lawn. Her eyes sweep the lawn and the house and the lawn again. The yard sale sign at the edge of the grass is a hand drawn sign, black marker on poster board taped to a yardstick and stuck in the ground. It says: Yard Sale, Today, Now.

The customer

The customer, the only one at 6:30 a.m., is not looking for anything in particular. She holds up a man's blazer. It is in good condition, a deep brown mocha color. There is no price tag.

"How much?" she asks.

The large old woman frowns and shakes her head. "Not for sale."

"Not for sale?"

"Not for sale." The woman takes the coat from the customer, tosses it on one of the theater seats. She looks toward the house, turns back. "Not for sale," she says.

The customer goes to the trees. She stands looking at the photographs. Roses. A rose and a rose and a rose and count, nine, nine framed photographs of a rose. They are all the same.

She stares intently, trying to see differences. A rose. Again and again and again. Even the frames are the same. She picks one up and raises it toward the woman.

"Not for sale," the woman says.

"But…"

"No," she says and strides toward the customer. "No," she whispers and grabs the photograph, puts it down against the tree. "No."

"But…"

The customer is puzzled. She has other stops. Her coffee is getting cold in the car. There is nothing to be purchased here.

She is walking away when the smaller, younger woman runs out of the house. She is yelling, shouting in what the customer thinks is Spanish, but not. Portuguese maybe. Something lovely, except the woman's voice is shrill and the older woman is waving her hand, erasing the younger woman's shouts.

"Wait," the small woman says. She runs to the customer. "You want things?" she asks. The customer can see this woman has been crying. Her eyes are red, her short hair and cheeks damp, as if she has just washed her face.

"Well," the customer hesitates and the small woman says, "Buy it all. Whatever you want. Ignore her. My mother-in-law," she says with a wave at the gypsy woman. "She cannot let go."

Letting Go

The small woman is the wife of the man, the photographer, whose belongings are being sold. Or not sold. The man has left; he has gone to Iceland, where it is green, he said, to work. To take photographs, to make art. He said he must, even though his wife would not go. She did not want to go to Iceland and when he called a week ago to say he had found love in Iceland, she decided she would rid herself of this man who had found green love.

The old woman does not much like her son's wife, whom she thinks is small and childish and prone to weeping. She does not want this woman to sell her son's things, though he has said he will not return.

The wife says they are hers to sell.

Bargaining

"Well," the customer says. "I was looking at this rose." She picks up one of the prints. Perhaps not the same one she first chose. She doesn't know.

"Yes, we have nine. Do you want all nine?"

The customer frowns and looks to her car. She should have brought her coffee with her. She thinks maybe a headache is starting. She wonders why no other customers have pulled up. She looks down the street. She sees a man in his bathrobe bending slowly to pick up his newspaper from his driveway.

"All of them. Five dollars," the smaller woman says.

"It isn't right," the old woman shouts. She sits in a theater seat, the brown coat on her legs. She picks at threads. "It isn't right," she shouts again.

The smaller woman shouts back, "Quiet! Why don't you leave?" When she turns back to the customer, her eyes are tearing up again. "I am sorry," she says. "Four dollars."

"But they are all the same," the customer says.

Or Not

The man, the photographer, the husband, the son, would argue that they are not the same. He would say each shot was taken when he was in a different frame of mind. He would laugh at his pun. Happiness. Fatigue. Excitement. He would say he knows which rose is which. He would think he knows. He might.

The customer does not know which rose she holds. If she did know this about the man's roses, she would worry. She would not want the rose of sorrow. Or fear.

But the customer does not know this, and the young woman does not say anything and the older woman is still picking at the brown coat and someone is pulling up now in a green van and the photographer himself is in Iceland and in love.

Getaway

The customer thinks she will take the rose. Just one. She will offer a dollar. She is about to speak, when the older woman stands, puts the coat back on the chair, and begins walking toward the new customer, a bearded man who is bending, looking through the books. The younger woman yells, "No!" and she hurries toward the older woman and the two begin shouting again. The customer decides this is her chance to leave. Her coffee is waiting. She puts the rose down and scurries to her car. She has other sales to go to.

Later, the customer is home. She has spent the morning searching, rummaging. She is never sure what she will find or what she wants. Today she bought a set of pretty green glasses painted with yellow butterflies. Four of them. She washes one, which is all she really needs, just one, and she fills it with water. She sits on her couch and stares at the wall before her.

Perhaps it was the rose of hope she held in her hands. She does not know this. Only the man would know this. He could tell her which rose she would want. But he is in Iceland. The customer looks at the wall and thinks that tomorrow she will go back to the house. She will knock on the door and offer to buy.

After Carlos the Continuity Expert Quit the Movie and Headed to Costa Rica

He said it had to do with birds. They had names, beautiful names, and he'd call them out like he was reciting prayer: *scarlet-thighed dacnis, chestnut-headed oropendola*. The women on the set found it erotic, the way he said these names, but one day he was saying *thrush-like schiffornis* and then he was gone. He left a message on the director's answering machine. She showed up for the filming of the diner scene for *Emilio's Girls* and scowled a lot and drank enough coffee that her hands shook. Someone gave her a muscle relaxer, which helped.

Scenes were shot. Again. Again. Days of shooting. Not great shots. The actors said it was the moon, the stars, the time of year, the ghosts from *Scooby-Doo.*

Without Carlos things happened.

Ivy, who played the diner owner, wore a pale pink lipstick and then it was a darker mauve. One day she had a long red welt running up her arm. When asked, she would say it was from a cat. Ivy would not say that it was her husband, come to visit during the filming, and she would not say that it was a fight and that she had scratched herself along a wall after he pushed her. She was in love and that wouldn't do at all.

In earlier shots, Vera, the waitress, had a pencil in hand and one tucked behind her ear. Later, the pencil behind the ear was missing; it had fallen somewhere, along with crumbs from a blueberry muffin she ate during a break even though she was on a low carb diet.

When Vera asked, "What can I get you?" Emilio sipped from his water glass. In some shots, he was empty handed when he said the line "But there is only you" to Yvette, the woman sitting across from him. In some shots the water glass was full. In some it was half empty. Emilio complained that he thought the water tasted metallic, that someone was trying to poison him, though the food service folks said the water was bottled.

Julia, the director, who also wrote and starred in the film, looked on the verge of weepy. She did not have a huge budget. She had vision and drive but not enough backing, she said to the hair stylist.

Billy, the hair stylist, was young and handsome and in love with Emilio. He wanted to do a good job, but he disliked Yvette, who was playing the new girlfriend. People assumed that off the set, Yvette was having an affair with Emilio—the way she fawned, the way she sat with her knee touching his even though the script did not direct her to. If asked, Billy would say it was not intentional—the awkward switch of the part in Yvette's hair—right side on Tuesday, left on Wednesday, but people would still wonder.

Frank, Billy's lover, was the wardrobe coordinator, and he didn't like the way Billy looked at Emilio. He knew a crush when he saw one, and he was so busy complaining about it to Vera between takes, that he overlooked certain details. Emilio's shirt was unbuttoned two buttons in some scenes, three in others. There were sunglasses tucked in his shirt pocket. Sometimes.

There were other issues too.

The clock wasn't reset and time didn't match so that when Julia entered the diner, strode over to Emilio and Yvette and said, "You left home six weeks ago and here you are?" it was 10:37 on the clock on the wall and it was 4:20 when she strode out after slapping Emilio with her purse. Too long to be in the diner, even if the peach cobbler was the best in town.

There was mustard on the table and then there wasn't. The flowers by the diner door were blooming on Tuesday and drooping by late Wednesday afternoon.

Things happened. Continuity was lost. Each take did not match the previous one. The actors had anxiety attacks, the director had a migraine, the cameraman's teenage daughter was in drug rehab.

A countertop with three dishes, a countertop swept clean. Details some moviegoers would later catch. They would chuckle and feel smart and post comments on websites.

What they wouldn't pinpoint or mention, because they did not know, was this: the human heart could not be held to continuity. It did what it wanted.

Julia had a postcard from Carlos hidden in a dresser drawer. It was addressed to the cast and crew of *Emilio's Girls*. On the front was a rainforest scene. His note on the back said many things and mentioned the sighting of a *rufous motmot*. Julia read his cramped writing almost daily. She fanned her tears with the postcard until it warped and crinkled. No matter.

She knew the words by heart. They never changed.

Request for Refund

I'm not sure why it's necessary to fill out this form when at some places customer satisfaction is of the utmost importance. Like at the grocery store. If I stop in and say, "These apples have no taste," the customer service person smiles and takes the bag of apples and gives me my money back. Even if I don't have a receipt. Well, unless it's that one mean girl with the red hair and insane amount of freckles. The point is, I could have bought those apples anywhere and easily returned them. Yet here I am filling out a form that requires an explanation detailing why I want a refund for a community education class. "Learning for life enhancement"—so says the catalog.

My English teachers drilled the persuasive essay into my head. So I know the format. Thesis, supports, conclusion. But what I'd really like to write is a one-sentence statement: I WAS NOT SATISFIED WITH THE CLASS. However, the office secretary (who rivals Grocery Freckle Face in the crappy personality department) says that since I've completed the six-session course I can't get a refund. But I can petition and fill out form 34RMB. And form 34RMB asks for a detailed explanation, so I suppose I could follow an essay format and start with a thesis statement.

Danny Gilbert's Songwriting for Guitar Players class sucked.

Three reasons: 1. The guy with bad allergies and awful lyrics about Juanita. 2. A lack of artistic understanding by my classmates. 3. Danny Gilbert's failure to recognize my talent.

The truth is, I could go off on more than three reasons, and I would, except I know I should stay focused. I remember my English teachers said that—stay focused and don't ramble when trying to make a point. Which, honestly, is ridiculous, because my favorite teachers were the ones who did ramble because then they were interesting. Like Mrs. Vettle. She used to tell us about how she was in love with Keith Richards. She'd write him love letters. Once he wrote back. She wouldn't bring the letter to school because it was framed and hanging in her house. I think she used to get high in the faculty parking lot during lunch.

Then there was Mrs. Welch. She should have gotten high in the parking lot and lost a bit of focus because then she'd have been more interesting. People would have listened instead of writing notes and making weapons out of pencils and rubber bands and paperclips. Maybe then she wouldn't have had that breakdown in the middle of Anatomy class. One second she was holding the femur of Scott the Skeleton and the next she was crying. She grabbed her purse from a filing cabinet and ran out. We never saw her again. We had a sexy substitute for the rest of the year—Mr. Bosworth—and I really did learn anatomy then. Ask me anything. Tibia, fibula, metatarsals.

May I add that my request for a refund is not about the money. I mean, $45 for a six-session class isn't bad. Not like when I took the candle making class. That cost $45 plus a $30 materials fee for wax and dyes and scents, and I could never get my candles to smell like much—definitely not like blueberry muffins or cinnamon vanilla harvest. For Danny Gilbert's class, all we needed was a guitar, which I had. I bought it at a garage sale months ago. Cost me $20 but the woman threw in a strap and a stand—and a beer that I drank with her. I thought it would be the kind of moment I could later write about. Which I did. I performed that song during Danny Gilbert's class. I was told it had potential, and I'm going to take that as a positive even though nobody clapped madly like they did for Honking Nose. Anyway, the refrain was the best part, so I'll give an example, which I know is important in defending a point:

The beer was cold and so was my heart
The guitar at my feet was there as part
Of a daylight moment in a daydream time
And I'm buyin' myself an easy rhyme.

So that song, which is pretty awesome, got this "has potential" comment. Meanwhile, Honking Nose—the guy with bad allergies—well he had a song that was in no way close to awesome. It was this slow sad ballad about his old girlfriend Juanita. It didn't have the heartfelt cosmic absurdity that my songs have, and it didn't sound like the sort of song Danny Gilbert would like. I've seen Danny perform more than a dozen times. Never did he play anything as lame as "Juanita Leave the Light On." God-awful. *"Juanita leave the light on so I can look in your eyes, see the look of surprise, when I walk out the front door."* But everyone went wild for it. The class clapped and clapped and Danny Gilbert said, "That was really good, man."

That got me. I mean, the class wasn't all that bright—I won't even get started on Hortense Manfred who had this annoying habit of shushing everyone if we were tuning up or picking out a C note while Danny was talking. I know Danny is hot, and I should have been the one shushing people, but Hortense took it upon herself to be the shusher. She was probably fifty years old. She was up there at the front of the little classroom, practically in Danny's lap. Like she wanted to take him home with her—and she was old enough to be his mother! I'm just using Hortense as an example of the type of people in this class. There was also the husband and wife who were trying to make their marriage work, bonding through community education. I don't think it was working. You could hear them bickering in the hallway before class started. And there was a fourteen-year-old boy who sang songs about Armageddon. Sometimes his voice cracked.

So anyhow, after Honking Nose got that clap and "really good, man," he felt so great that he offered to buy everyone beers at Riley's when we were done. Of course I took him up on the offer, and I remembered to call him Miles instead of Honking Nose. I even asked him what he did for a living, nice polite conversation, and he told me how he owned a bakery.

All this is digression, but supportive. Can digression be supportive? I think so. And I know a less than enthusiastic "this has potential" is not enough to warrant a refund. Honestly, I know my songs were the best in the class. If not "Garage Sale Guitar," well then surely, "Airport Hibachi," which I wrote while I was sitting—yes—in an airport. Let me give you an example from "Airport Hibachi" because I'm very proud of it:

Gotta get the grill and make a steak
Plane's delayed and my mind's awake
Too much coffee, not enough beer
Dyin' to get myself out of here
Guy walking by with a cape round his neck
Doesn't make sense, oh what the heck
Use my blues like a marinade sauce
One day you'll see it's your own damn loss.

So after I played that song in Danny Gilbert's Songwriting for Guitar Players class, the people clapped. A polite clap. Danny said, "Nice," but the way he said it I knew he didn't mean it. He sounded tired, which made me think he wasn't enjoying this teaching gig. Danny's a star in this town. I mean, he's in a band called Squirrels with Binoculars. They do some touring around this part of the state, and they play to packed bars. Danny has a sweet bluesy voice. The way he plays guitar and looks up at the audience with this real soft smile makes my heart melt. But I've never been one of those groupie girls, like this one girl I know. Catherine. She wears the tightest skirts and tank tops, and she dances real close to the stage. I think she sleeps with a lot of guys. I don't know for sure because I don't really know her. I just know she works as a waitress at the Ink Stain, this cruddy little restaurant I like because it's close to my house. Anyhow, Danny Gilbert is a guitar god in my book, and when I heard he was teaching a community ed class, I had to sign up. I knew I could wow him with my own talent. Then we might be able to have a real relationship, not some sleazy one.

But that didn't happen. Obviously. Otherwise I wouldn't be writing this request, and I wouldn't have to sit here and pretend I don't notice Little Miss Secretary glaring at me. Probably because it's almost five o'clock and she wants to go home and drink a big glass of wine, which is what I'm thinking it's time to do. So I need to conclude. Plus my hand is cramping from trying to write all this on 34RMB. As you can see, I've used the back of the form. Anyhow, a summation:

Heretofore (now that is one ridiculous word), and really what I mean is, in conclusion, I would like to request a refund for Danny Gilbert's class. I wasn't adequately supported, and I don't feel like it helped me to "crank out new tunes" as was mentioned in the course description. If a monetary refund cannot be accommodated, I will also accept a credit so I may take

Adam Simon's Creative Writing class. I heard him do a reading from his new novel last week at the bookstore. Let me just say I was very impressed.

Juan Tomás and the Pale Yellow Letters

Check-in

When Suzy had her breakdown, she left her fiancé in the backyard tossing rye grass seed. She drove herself two turnpike exits over to the nearest hotel and got herself a room. Queen-sized bed, coffee maker, small refrigerator, cable television, pool view. She cranked the air conditioning to cold, took off her shoes and dropped down on the bed. Suzy stared at the painting of two blue jays on a sun-soaked front porch railing. She imagined she heard waving grass and wooden porch planks creaking in the late afternoon wind.

Later she cried, watched a movie halfway through before she turned to a home decorating show and realized she had to call her fiancé. But she couldn't. She couldn't explain why she left him—there was nothing wrong with him—but she knew it was the nothingness that made her finally pack a small bag while he tossed rye seed. She didn't love him enough. People would want something bigger, but that was it. She didn't love him enough.

She holed up for three days.

She noticed things.

The hotel had a game room with an old version of Ms. Pac-Man, a meeting/conference room where Perpetual Insurance employees wore khakis and sensible shoes, an empty exercise room, and a spa where you could get a one-hour massage. She considered the massage more than once, but figured with all that kneading and touching, she might just fall apart.

The pool area had a bar called Lounge Chair Louie's. Happy Hour was from four to seven. The tiki hut was big enough for a bar, a television, and six round tables with chairs. It was usually crowded, even when it wasn't Happy Hour, and the bartender wore a Hawaiian shirt and a cowboy hat. Mixed messages. Aloha and giddy-up. The music in Lounge Chair Louie's was Jimmie Buffet and old Eighties pop and the television played ESPN without sound.

Suzy watched the maids shuffle along the hallways and the Europeans with their sunburned legs and sandaled toes flipflop around the pool area. She saw mothers rolling their tired eyes at chlorine-juiced children while fathers put their sunglasses on so they could look at the cabana girls. She saw families wearing Mickey Mouse ears and Mickey Mouse t-shirts; she saw a bandana-headed man carrying a beer, a leather journal, and a book of Dylan Thomas poems, and she figured he was writing about woe and wonder. She saw a handsomely beautiful transvestite lose an eyelash in the lobby, and she saw three teenagers drinking wine coolers. She saw a woman with a dog in her handbag.

It was that kind of hotel.

On her third night there, she was sitting on her private terrace that overlooked the pool, drinking a glass of white wine from a bottle she had bought at the convenience store down the street, when she heard a man's voice. It was slow and deep. The voice was coming from the next terrace over.

"This is one of my favorites," he said.

She listened to the man read a story to his lover, who every once in awhile said things like "Go on" and "How sad," until she heard the man's voice stop, she heard chairs scrape on the concrete floor and the two go inside. The story wasn't finished.

Then Suzy heard the couple having loud sex. But what happened in the story? What happened to the farmer? Suzy tried to make up endings, but she had a hard time thinking about such a soft, tender story, the man's words, while she heard whimpers and moans and the bed sighing.

In the morning, she called her mother. She cancelled her wedding and moved back in with her parents.

The story

The days Suzy sat at her parents' pool, she watched the yellow duck with sunglasses that was actually a chlorine container float its way across the hours, and she tried to remember the story.

One morning a young farmer, Juan Tomás, woke to the sound of the rooster that strutted and preened in his front yard. That morning the farmer went to put his boots on, but when he picked up the right boot, the one with the heel worn down on one side, he saw that the boot was stuffed with a paper. He reached in his boot and pulled out a pale yellow envelope. When he opened it, he saw it was addressed only to "Mi Querida" and it was filled with love and sweetness and signed, Graciela. The letter smelled of vanilla and oranges and though the farmer did not know the name, Graciela,—ah, Graciela—it was beautiful and he thought she too must be beautiful, and so the farmer kept the letter in his shirt pocket while he worked his field that day, letting the words lift his heart so that he sang while he worked, letting the honeyed smell of vanilla and oranges perfume his own sweat. This happened for five days—the young farmer would wake and his right boot would have another love letter from Graciela, always yellow, always smelling of the same sweetness. On the eve of the fifth letter, the man woke in the night and heard singing, a soft song, and he could see no one in his small home, and so he closed his eyes and let the voice that was musical like spring rain lull him to sleep. The next day was the same. A letter of love and tenderness and poetry about the world and its grand beauty, the sky, the stars, the dance of midday clouds. In the morning a letter, in the evening, a song.

On the seventh night, the farmer woke and heard the soft singing and it seemed to be moving through the room, it seemed to dance about his doorway, and then he heard it outside. He decided to follow the song, for surely it was Graciela asking him to come meet her in the moonlight, under the blooming cottonwood tree in his front yard.

When he went out into the chilled night, however, there was no one, nothing but the crescent moon like a wing in the sky, the distant stars. The singing seemed to fade slowly, then disappear altogether.

"Graciela is the one singing," the woman on the hotel terrace had said to her lover.

"Yes," he said, and Suzy imagined the licking of a finger, the turning of the page.

"Go on," the woman prompted. "Tell me."

"Later," the man said. And Suzy heard the scraping of chairs on the concrete terrace floor and a giggle from the woman and the sound of the sliding glass door opening and closing.

An Explanation

Suzy told her own love story, or love-less story, to a friend over dinner. Months after she left the hotel, the two women sat in a new local bistro where the menu was printed on pale parchment and the choices included herb pesto with chicken and seared salmon with roasted new potatoes and Portobello mushroom on sourdough. Suzy finally ordered the field greens salad sans goat cheese. She tried to ignore the waitress with the too-cute mole and the raised-eyebrows look of disdain—oh, just the salad—and instead she turned to her friend and said, "I just couldn't marry him." On the wood-paneled wall alongside their table were photographs by a local artist—a series of black and white prints of up close and out of focus nudes. In between squints to see if the photos would come clear, Suzy told her story. She punctuated it with "I just don't know" and "Know what I'm saying?" and sips of wine.

When her friend stopped spooning her butternut squash bisque and said, "But he was such a nice guy," Suzy made fitful stabs at endive and butter lettuce.

Squint, a man's backside in moonlight.

Squint, a woman's shoulders softened, vulnerable.

"You know that feeling where you know the ending? And that just makes you sad?" Suzy lifted the almost empty wine glass, tilted it so that the wine had the chance to spill, but didn't.

"It just wasn't enough," she said.

Possibilities

The farmer story could have many endings: perhaps infinite—fires and ghost boots and cowgirl bandits and jaguar visions and twin bodies and witches and devil water dreams and all manner of plotlines. When Suzy considered endings, she tried to remember the scent of vanilla and orange. She looked up cottonwood trees online, since there were only palms and bottlebrush dipping and curtsying in her yard. She learned that the cottonwood seeds were dispersed in downy white tufts, that spring breezes would blow the seeds for miles.

She thought of cotton puffs tumbling and afloat like clouds across long fields; she considered the smell of ripe fruit, the sound of love songs. It became a game, a way to pass time. Tell the story, tell a new ending. She was curious—this endless tale—and she supposed she would never know.

Years later, in her lover's bed

There was the small breeze through the opened window, so light it stirred nothing, and there was the distant hush-hush-hush of waves. She woke early, with the bluegray and pale gold of late dawn. Her lover slept beside her. Her hand on his chest, she could measure the rise and fall of body, the even breaths in and out. She could feel the smooth line of the scar above his left nipple; she could hear the faint whistle of his sleep.

She turned from her side to her back and watched the leisurely spin of the ceiling fan. She thought flower, star, wings, flower.

Her lover slept beside her and so she slid out of bed quietly, grabbed his robe from the back of an old wingback chair, and while wrapping it around her, she saw on the floor at the side of his bed, a book. It was a hardback book and the title, there in bold black type: *Juan Tomás and the Pale Yellow Letters and Other Stories.*

Not possible. She had heard the tale almost three years ago. The unfinished story.

Suzy bent down, reaching for the book she figured could be illusion. But no, it was solid, the weight of words and stories a real thing, and so she picked it up and she left her lover sleeping. She went into his kitchen and sat.

And the rest

On the eighth day the farmer woke and he could not remember if he had really left his bed to stare up at the moon, to listen for a woman's soothing lullaby. He bent to pick up his boot and there was no letter. He checked the other boot. No letter. He was so pained, a morning without his Graciela, without the endearments, without the promise of love, that he could not eat his morning tortilla, and he did not want his morning coffee. He sat there, instead, reading the old letters that he had wrapped in a shawl worn thin by time. He did not go to his field, but let day wander into dusk into night. He slept restlessly, listening to silence.

At daybreak, the farmer heard the voice, the beautiful singing, like small bells or a woman's giggle caught in the cupping of a hand, and he rose and walked barefoot to his doorway and out into the dawn. He heard the rustle and flutter of the cottonwood leaves and he watched them twist in the day's first wind. And then there, in a lower branch of the tree, perched in a haze of white, a bird, a pale yellow bird with eyes of the darkest black ink. As Juan Tomás wiped his tired eyes, he realized the bird was indeed made of paper, the bird was a bird of pale yellow letters, and he finally spoke her name, "Graciela," and with his voice, which ruffled the tree leaves and made the little bird cock its head, the pale yellow bird beat its paper wings and was gone. The farmer watched as the bird disappeared in the gray distance. He stood there, for quite a long time, staring as the sky lifted, as blue morning settled, and he wondered if this was all a sign of good or bad to come.

Endings may still leave us wondering

Suzy did not return to the bedroom for a long time. She made coffee, she sat and stared at the refrigerator, which her lover had decorated with postcards—Brazil, Crete, Maui, Cancun—and free magnets from pizza chains and grocery lists he never took with him. She listened to the gurgle and lonely hiss of the coffee maker. She noticed objects on the windowsill over the sink: an old milk bottle filled with marbles, a blown glass hummingbird, a mango ripening—yellow, orange, red. She picked the mango up to smell it, the dark sweetness escaping its thick skin. She ran a finger over the book cover, her finger sketching the letters slowly, precisely, the swing of the J, the hook of the U.

She was happy she had not heard the ending years ago. She was happy she had not heard it that night on the terrace when she was sad and scared and the people down below were bellowing melancholy ballads with unending refrains at Lounge Chair Louie's.

Suzy carried the book back to her lover's bedroom. He was still sleeping. She did not want to wake him. He slept on his back, legs apart, head to the side. The mid-morning light through the slightly-opened window blinds crisscrossed his body, rays of shadow and not shadow, so that her lover was grayness and white, focused and blurred simultaneously.

Scarlet

I want a boy with a red truck, a boy with a black dog he lets ride in the back of the truck. I want this boy who wears flip flops on Saturdays, and maybe sometimes cowboy boots on Fridays, but not the shiny ones with really pointy toes, no not those, and sometimes the black dog sleeps curled on the front porch of his house, which is on acres of land, and there's a book and a bottle of red wine on a table on the porch, right next to a rocking chair, where he sat reading and drinking, right before he got in his truck to come pick me up, and when I run out the front door and hop in next to the boy who smells like fire and soap, I tell him I've painted my toenails scarlet just for him, and we head down to the overlook, where we lie down on an old quilt that I won't ask about, and we watch the stars and he points out constellations because he knows things about earth and water and sky, and he asks if it's all right if he kisses me, and I say yes even though I should say no, and later he asks, "What is it you like about me?" and I say, "Your truck," and he says, "No, tell me," and I say, "Your dog," and he says, "You aren't telling the truth," and I say, "It's too late for that."

Vibe

There's an old manuscript.

It sits in a file folder marked *In Progress* though the folder has not been touched in years. This is not progress. Or perhaps it is. The writer has ignored the folder all these years. Maybe it is the writer who is *in progress*. Hopefully.

She has written new manuscripts, some of which are also in folders. Some of the folders are marked with story titles, some are unmarked or doodled on. She likes to draw geometric doodads, they meander across things and turn back on themselves. Flowers too. She draws flowers with pointy petals and within the petals are the geometric designs. There are folders with this—flowers and triangles and zigzag lines.

She has written new manuscripts and some of these manuscripts are not in folders. They are on the floor or they are in the recycling box or they are on the old futon mattress picking up dog hairs. Some of the manuscripts are scrap paper. Those have doodles on them.

But there is this one manuscript in the *In Progress* folder. A good story. Poorly written, or maybe well-written, but written ten years ago and the writer is ten years older and more critical.

Here is the first line: *There was the sound of laughter, flirtation, the clink of bottles on banisters, and then Earl Bisquitwater walked out on stage, saxophone held high, and he pumped it up in the air, like a cheerleader with a pompom, and the crowd, maybe fifty people, started moving toward him.*

The writer realizes her style has not changed much.

Here is the last line: *Images flashed in quick succession: the young dancer out on the town, eating at some late night sub shop, Earl, sitting in a van, traveling through the dark night, May, sleeping, waiting for her husband to come home, the bartenders wiping tables and bagging bottles, and...*

Oh. The last line is horrible. It is one of those long, meandering sentences she is guilty of. The writer realizes this is not the original last line. The manuscript before her—with its dog-eared corners and the half-moon coffee stain—is a newer one, not the first or second draft of the story. She wonders what happened to the earlier draft, where the last scene is Earl and his van and the young dancer giving the peace sign. That version is not in the *In Progress* folder.

She skims the story quickly. Yes this version has a new point of view, an audience member, a young woman; it is not the impersonal third person, it is not the story of Earl, but the story of the young woman watching Earl.

It is closer to the truth, this newer version. It is maybe not even ten years old. Maybe six or seven.

But still.

The story is problematic. Maybe not one to be worked on. Maybe one to be put back in the *In Progress* folder, put back in the filing cabinet. Maybe the story behind the story is better.

Here's the story behind the story.

The writer went to a bar with her boyfriend. She was on acid. On acid, there is nothing mundane. Or the mundane is fascinating in its mundane-ness. And so the writer was in a bar, which was really a gutted old theatre, no seats, just a stage for musicians and two bars along the walls and sticky sloping floors. And this is where the writer saw Earl, whose name is not really Earl, but the writer will not tell the real name, because the writer worries about things, and she doesn't wish to worry about the real Earl knowing that she has supposed or imagined his life.

Because this is what she's done. This is what "Vibe" is about. A writer supposing a musician's life and the writer writing about a woman wondering about the musician. Well, in the later draft, which is now in front of her, this is what she did. In the earlier draft, there was no woman in the audience wondering about Earl. There was just Earl and the writer writing about Earl. But that draft, it seems, is gone.

But the story behind the story. The writer was on acid and so nothing was mundane and some things were funny and some were scary but the particulars are so many years old that it is hard to even know anything. But the writer does know that Earl came out on stage and he had an orchestra, or a very large band with him, and the music they played was jazz, Coltrane and Davis and Coleman all fused together, and the writer had not heard this sort of thing before, and she was shocked, profoundly shocked that the noise became music.

The story is not about the music. It is about the man. Earl. Because the man, who played saxophone and flute and maybe even a trumpet, was the perfect character, with his hoots and hollers and his hands waving and flapping and his strutting across the stage and his bird calls and whistles and then those moments when he played and the sound just got loud and wicked and delirious.

This is what the writer wrote: *He wiped his brow with the handkerchief he had in the breast pocket of his baggy maroon suit, and then he shouted "Kick it!" and the drums began, the brass, the sounds forcing their way into the crowd.*

The writer had thought, this man has a story. I can tell the story.

And so she went home and wrote about Earl and his dying wife and how this was his last show, in the tiny bar with the crazy guy dancing in front and the young woman who stood at the back and watched it all.

And here is what happened outside the story. Ten years later, the writer is in a music store, and she sees a CD by Earl, whose real name is not Earl. He is still playing. He is making music and CD's and a photo of his face is there on the back cover, and his saxophone is there too, and not his wife, because maybe she did die, or maybe she's just not around, or maybe she took the picture, or maybe he doesn't even have a wife named May who had asked him to stop playing, stop gigging and come home. And all this speculation makes the writer buy the CD, and she takes it home and puts it on the stereo, and there is something about it that makes her remember, but not really as much as she'd like. She wonders what happened to the crazy dancer, what happened to the girl's boyfriend. She knows what happened to the girl. And she knows that most of the time, our lives are not what we dream them up to be.

And the writer looks at the old manuscript and realizes she still does not know what to do with the story. Some stories are like that. They are hard to tell.

What to Do on a Saturday Night One Week after Your Lover Announced, "Sayonara, Sweetheart," Even Though He's Not Japanese and He Never Called You Sweetheart Before

Go to the bookstore and read books you won't buy. Try not to bend or curl the paperback covers. Sit in a wingback chair and stare at all the people who go to a bookstore at night. See how the man in a wingback chair not far from you is curling the paperback cover of a fantasy novel. Hope he will buy the book and not just put it back on the shelf. Assume from his slouched posture, his easy smile, that he is delighted by warlocks and wizards and space travel, and remember that you are not. Be happy for this reader when a woman comes up behind him, taps her ringed hand on his head. Watch the two walk off. Sigh when you see he has left the book on the chair. Notice how some people look around nervously before they pick up something from erotica or self-help. Notice that the two sections are next to each other and assume that erotic self-help is the answer. Hope that you don't see anyone engage in erotic self-help in the bookstore. Consider checking out these sections before you leave.

Strum on your guitar. In your dimly-lit living room. Not in the bookstore. Decide to learn a new song and pull out your old songbook. First draw squiggly lines, smiley faces in the dust on the cover. Then pick a song at random. Try to play the guitar behind your head. Realize it isn't easy. Sing and croon and howl. Stand by the window and let your voice warble and flutter. Sing with other people in mind. Sing like Johnny Cash, then Frank Sinatra. Like Aretha Franklin. End with a Janis Joplin voice. People will hear you, even if you think they can't. Swish your hair around and throw yourself upon couch pillows. Consider that some neighbor thinks there is funny business going on in your apartment. Be happy that you have given someone something to talk about.

Move to the bedroom. Make a puppet with an old red sock. Sew button eyes. Two different buttons. One big black eye, one tiny pearly one. Draw the nose with a Sharpie. Make it a triangle nose like a jack-o-lantern and remember when Halloween was the greatest, when you dressed up as a princess, a hobo, a vampire, a gypsy.

Go to the hall closet and find the black lace shawl your grandmother sent you from Greece. Wrap it around your shoulders and finish your puppet. Yarn hair. Yellow. Avoid a blunt bob and cut the hair in jagged lines. Have the puppet talk like Madeline Kahn. Don't let it talk to you though. That would be crazy. Only allow it to talk to the air, the ceiling fan, the skylights, the moon as it crosses your window.

This Is Us

We've decided, my friends and I, to start our own reality show. We say this because we are funny and because we've just finished another round of banter that involved the word "chicken" and another word that I won't mention because we are just too weird. Then again, weird is what will sell our show.

I'm lying. When I say we, I mean I, because I'm the one who said, "We need our own show." Nobody else agreed with me because most of us are annoyed by reality television.

Opening credit sequence:

Eight of us, ages 32–40, are sitting on two couches around a cocktail table at Jenny and Jason's house and the music is playing and it's Pink Floyd's "Careful With That Axe, Eugene." We like to do this sort of thing—get together and have dinner and get a little buzz going and listen to music. Zach, who is bearded and looks sort of like a bear, stands up and pounds his chest, and the rest of us ignore this because we're in the opening shot and we need to look like we are lost in thought. Which we are.

But honestly, I'm a little weirded out by the music because it gets a bit scary.

Variations on the opening:

I'm thinking it would be cool for the intro to change each week. Like maybe a different song would be playing, something not as scary as "Careful With That Axe, Eugene." And maybe we'd change our location too. Like sometimes we'd be sitting around on couches and sometimes on chairs on the front porch. Maybe once on the roof. Or in a swimming pool, all of us sitting underwater. And maybe someone different would stand up each week and do something unusual like how Zach just did that chest pounding thing. Pirouette. Jumping jacks. Warrior II pose. Statue of Liberty. I'm a Little Tea Pot. The week we're underwater, someone could do Martha Washington hair.

"In our new reality show, each week we could use a different song," I say. "Everyone gets to pick one."

Oh yeah! Now they're interested. We're talking music. Which leads to a discussion of what type of song would work in an opening about us. Finally, I've reeled them in. But not really. We have jobs to keep.

What goes on for the 22 minutes we're on the air:

We sit around and talk and laugh and sometimes someone does something funny as shit and then we all laugh harder and we riff off each other and we use a joke until it is basically dead. There isn't real drama because we're not about to put that stuff out there on television.

I suggest that maybe the show should be about how we wish we were a band but we aren't and maybe we could be even though some of us aren't great. We have a saxophonist and an oboe player and a banjo picker and a fiddler and a didgeridoo dude and two guitarists. One air guitarist.

And while I'm trying to hype this idea up, I realize one by one, everyone is leaving the room, heading to the kitchen because dessert is ready and we need to go get forks and plates and spear some key lime pie.

Closing shot and random end clip:

I'm left all alone on the couch and now something like Herbie Hancock's "Chameleon" is on the stereo.

My head involuntarily does this groovy bob and sway, and I think it's a great ending sequence for our show. How everyone walks away and sort of fades out like ghosts as they leave the room and then there's only one person left. And tonight it's me and I just close my eyes and sink deeper into the couch because nobody is watching except our camera person and because this is reality TV and this is what I do. The screen goes to black.

But then there will be a weird little clip tacked on at the end, something old school, cartoon, but completely foolish. Maybe a rocking chair with a small cupcake sitting in it. The rocking chair rocks and the cupcake falls off and then there's a word written in all caps like SPLAT! and a really cute voice says Splat! out loud and giggles. Because onomatopoeia is cool. And I just want everyone to be happy.

Cardboard Ben

Nikki thought she had a reason for walking out of Moondog's Record House with a smaller-than-life-size cardboard cutout of Ben Stevens, lead singer and guitarist for The Howler Monkeys.

She knew the real Ben Stevens. Not knew him like all his fans, the women who wore tiny tees and tight jeans and danced with arms in the air and probably shouted "Rock on!" at any famous musician. And not knew him like the people who read about him in the magazines, those folks who knew he was a Sagittarius and his favorite color was orange.

Nikki knew him from junior high and high school. She knew Ben Stevens broke his arm doing bike tricks off a ramp he had built in his driveway. She knew that only a few people signed his cast because he wasn't popular. He was sort of a weird guy.

And Nikki also knew Ben Stevens had been in Mr. Denslow's twelfth grade English class and that one day he turned around to her and said, "Keats is wicked cool," and she had to gulp and agree because here was this guy she'd been crushing on for years and he had turned around and revealed a truth, a philosophical observation that she was pretty sure he wouldn't say to just anyone. Keats was cool. She knew Ben Stevens had an old red Honda, and he was the features editor for the Bivens High monthly newspaper, and Ben Stevens was very serious about deadlines so Nikki always tried to have her articles done on time. And she knew Ben Stevens dated Abigail Armstrong, a swimmer, until he headed to Chapel Hill and that was the last she'd heard.

Until, of course, Ben Stevens made it in the indie music world. Then he had posters in the record store and he looked very much the same as he had fifteen years ago, the day of graduation when he had given Nikki a quick hug and said "Good luck out there."

She did finally explain this all to—she looked at his nametag—Trevor, the college boy who was working the front counter at Moondog's Record House. She had to really, because there was no way she could walk out the door with Cardboard Ben and not be noticed. She had contemplated it, pretending he was real, her arm slung around his waist as she shuffled toward the exit, but it seemed so ludicrous, foolish, and really, she just couldn't get in trouble with the law. She was a public servant, a schoolteacher. How could she go to work and tell the kids, "Don't steal each other's lunchbags," if she herself had taken a cardboard cutout of a rock star? It was bad enough that she had tattoos—one on her ankle and one on her left hip (not that the kids knew about that one).

"Ben Stevens could have been my boyfriend," she told Trevor. "I was just too shy. You understand, don't you?" She looked at him and realized he didn't understand. Trevor was hot and Trevor had that laid back surfer boy look—hair bleached almost white by the sun and one of those hemp choker necklaces that basically said to the world: "I have sex in camping tents and Volkswagen pop up vans several times a year."

"Sure," he said. "Go ahead and take him."

"But…" Nikki paused. She hadn't expected it to be easy. She was ready to explain, to tell the tale of Ben Stevens, a story of unrequited love. "It was like, I was so nervous around him that I babbled. Once he told me I talked too much."

"Lady. Take him."

"Okay, thanks." But she hesitated at the counter. "I had this thing for him when he was the new kid. Came to our school and pretty much kept to himself."

"Cool."

Nikki could tell Trevor did not think it was cool. That Trevor didn't care. "Do you like Ben Stevens and the Howler Monkeys?"

Trevor shrugged. "Not my style. Sort of mainstream."

"Mainstream?"

"Yeah. His guitar playing isn't really stellar. It's passable."

"So why do you guys have a cutout of the guy if he's not stellar?"

"Look around. We put up whatever comes in."

"Won't anyone notice Cardboard Ben Stevens is gone?" Nikki felt slight disappointment.

"Maybe," Trevor said. "Weird shit happens here. One night we found somebody's swim goggles in the Classical section. Another time someone stole all the sheet music for John Prine songs, but left 'Angel from Montgomery.'"

"That doesn't make sense."

"No, it doesn't."

"Okay then," Nikki said. "I should be going."

"Yep."

"For your biographies," she told her sixth graders, "I want you to find some interesting facts about the person you've chosen. More than date of birth and who they married. Things that make your person seem *real.* Do you understand?"

She looked at her students. Twenty-three kids, all staring at her. Maybe fifteen of them listening. She hoped.

"Can you give us an example?" asked Willow.

"An example," Nikki said. "How many of you know Ben Stevens?"

She waited. The kids frowned, shook their heads. Willow raised her hand partially, waving it like she sort of knew.

"Willow?"

'He owns Ben & Jerry's?"

"Um, no," Nikki said. "He's a musician. He's got a band, the Howler Monkeys."

"Bonobo monkeys like to have sex a lot," Cody said. He smiled and Jake smacked his desk and laughed. Other kids snickered.

Nikki paused. "Okay, true. But I said howler monkeys. Totally different."

The class giggled.

"Anyhow, what I was saying is Ben Stevens is a musician and he's sort of famous now and I knew him when he was a kid, well, a teenager, and so I could tell you about how in eighth grade Ben played left field for the Bivens Bears."

"That's not very interesting," Willow said.

"I play left field for the Cyclones," Victor said. "I'm the best player on the team."

"That's a lie," Raymond said.

"Okay, Ben Stevens has four bulldogs named after the Beatles," Nikki said. She waited. This she knew from an article in *Spin* magazine. She knew John was the fattest of the bulldogs. That Ben Stevens' wife, Michelle, took care of them when he was on the road.

"I know who the Beatles are," Karen said. "My dad really likes them."

"Good," Nikki said. "Reports due next Wednesday."

"I have a beagle," Willow said.

~

At home, Nikki talked to Cardboard Ben. She had him propped up in her living room, in the corner, like a tall plant.

"It's not like I think he's real," she told her friend Vivian on the phone. "It's more like I'm using him as a muse."

"As a muse for what?" Vivian asked. "A muse means you're doing something artistic."

"I am. I'm collaging."

"Stupid crafty shit."

"It's helping me. It's an activity book called *Collaging Your Spirit.*"

"It would be better if you said you were making out with Cardboard Ben. Don't trade love for crafts. That's what my grandmother did."

"Love you too. Bye," Nikki said and hung up.

"So Cardboard Ben," Nikki said. "It's not like I think you're listening, and I definitely am not talking to you because I think you're real. I'm just talking at you, just thinking out loud."

Nikki sat on her couch, cross-legged, eating Thai food. Her dog Max had one eye opened on Cardboard Ben.

"You know, I didn't even realize you were a musician. I mean, I think I knew you were taking guitar lessons in high school, but I didn't know you were serious. I thought you'd grow up and be a writer. A journalist. Then again, I thought I would too. I'm a teacher. But I get summers off. Just two more months to go."

She paused, put her plate on the beat up cocktail table and reached for the *Spin* magazine. She flipped through it and stopped on a dog-eared page.

"According to this article, you were in a band in college called Fresh Roasted Peanuts. You played at local bars and majored in English."

She put the magazine down. "Remember when you said Keats was wicked cool. I thought so too, I was just afraid to say so."

"So figurative language spices up writing," Nikki said to her class. "Do you know what I'm saying?"

"Yes." Lance always answered her.

"Simile. A comparison between two things usually not considered alike and using the word 'like' or 'as' to make the comparison. For example." She paused. "Okay, let's see. Okay, Ben Stevens' voice is like freshly sanded oak planks."

She looked at the class and smiled.

They stared at her.

"Miss West," Elyse finally said. "What's with you and this guy?"

"Yeah, what happened to Roger?" Maureen said.

"Roger is the past," Nikki said.

"So who is this Ben Stevens, Miss West?" Lance asked.

Nikki sighed again and twisted her hair into a bun, stabbing a pencil through it. "That's a good question, you guys."

Nikki stared at Cardboard Ben and made lists.

<u>Why Cardboard Ben Should Not Be In My House:</u>

1. It is weird.

   It makes me seem sad and pathetic and soon I'll get cats. Cats. Plural.

2. Ben probably doesn't even remember me.

   He is most likely a drug-addled freak who doesn't even really write his own songs. He probably buys his lyrics off the girls he sleeps with. He asks them to write him poems and then he takes their ideas and writes songs. How else to explain a song like "Wicked Lover Be Cruel and Cruel Again?"

3. It is a sad and pathetic (see number one) attempt to hold on to a past that was not so terrific. Enough said.

4. Ben is not inspiring me.

   In fact, he is starting to bother me, with his easy stance, hands always in his pockets, that small smile like he's totally content. And the way his glasses are falling down his nose and he doesn't—he can't!—even push them back up. These things are bothering me.

5. Ben makes Max nervous.

Why It's Actually Cool That I Have Cardboard Ben:

1. Nobody else does!

   Then again, maybe others have Bens. Definitely others have cardboard people. I was once at a party and there was a cardboard Marilyn Monroe wearing a green tinsel wig.

2. It's really no different from the neighbor who has this weird sculpture in his front yard.

   It's made of metal and it's painted bright Day-Glo colors. It's a sculpture of a dancing woman, and she's got her arms thrown in the air and really wild long orange curls. It's pretty cool, but sometimes I wonder why it's in his yard and not in his house. Late at night it can freak me out. Like I'm driving by and out of the corner of my eye I think someone is running toward me.

3. ?

   There's no cool reason to have Cardboard Ben in my living room. I am such a loser.

"Cardboard Ben, maybe the reason I took you is because I haven't done anything daring and different in so long. And even then, I didn't really have to steal you. I just took you and put you in my car. Trevor didn't even care. He said you were mainstream. He said you weren't stellar. My students don't know who you are and my friend Vivian thinks I've got some kinky thing going with you.

"Something isn't right here, C.B."

Hi Ben.

I saw your article in *Spin* magazine and thought I'd say hey. I was just checking out your band website and saw this email contact. So hello!

This is Nikki West. From Bivens High School. And Bivens Junior High. We were in some classes together. And on newspaper staff.

Anyway, nice to see that you've made a name for yourself. I never knew you were a musician. Very cool.

I'm a teacher. And I'm writing a novel, but nobody knows that. Except Max, my dog, and Roger, my ex-boyfriend. And you. Send some good luck vibes my way if you can.

Hope all is well.

Best,
Nikki

"Email is so stupid," Nikki told Vivian over a cup of bad coffee.

"Drunk emails are the worst. I sent several the other night."

"I didn't get one."

"I mean to old boyfriends. Lovers you think you might want to try again," Vivian said.

"Done that."

"Don't send to Roger."

"I don't. I mean, I've thought about it, but I haven't."

"Good."

"I sent one to Ben Stevens."

"Oh lord."

"I know I'm talking to you like I said I wouldn't, but Cardboard Ben, here's the truth. I'm bored. I've had the same job for eight years and I've lived in this same crappy little house on this crappy little street, and I keep finding the wrong guys, and once in awhile I think I should just get up and go—head to Thailand or Boulder or Key West. Start over. But then I get scared.

"Since you're just standing there, C.B., I'll tell you what happened. I had this boyfriend, Roger. We met in a Starbucks. I know, corporate and all, but I get these gift cards from my students. Anyhow, Roger said, 'It's nice to know your boyfriend will let you go with me to dinner tonight.' I didn't have a boyfriend.

"He was smooth, C.B. I won't get into details, but I went to dinner, and things just happened. Like I said, he was smooth. Told me I was brainy and sexy. Told me I should write the new novel. Told me to forget the other failed attempts and do it again.

"Thing is, C.B., he had another woman. I didn't realize it at first. He was a pretty private guy. I finally figured it out when he called me Flora while we were having sex. Flora was one of his 'friends' from the Radiology Department. He tried to play it off, said his mind was on department issues, but I'm brainy and sexy—I knew. Flora the whore. She was married no less.

"The guy was a jerk. Too detached and too full of shit. But I didn't see it then. Thing is, C.B., sometimes I still miss that asshole."

"The problem with email, C.B., is that it's addictive. Especially when you're waiting for a response. I mean, it's like playing the slot machines, from what I've heard because I've never been to Vegas. Doesn't really interest me, you know? But email, it's like that.

"For example, I just checked to see if Real Ben responded. He didn't. It could be though, that just three seconds ago Real Ben finally hit send and now if I check, I'll have an email. Then again, he's on tour and I'm sure very busy.

"That used to happen with Roger. I'd send an email and he wouldn't respond and then I'd wait and finally I'd call him and he'd say something like, 'I was working late.' Or 'I went to get some doughnuts.' It's honestly enough to make a person nuts."

~

"He's making me feel like a loser," Nikki told Vivian. They were eating Mexican food, scooping free chips into free salsa while they drank two-for-one margaritas.

"Only you can make yourself feel like a loser, Nik," Vivian said. "Didn't your *Collaging into the Spirit World* book tell you that?"

"Fuck you."

Reasons Why At This Point I Really Should Get Rid of Cardboard Ben:

1. I have to admit, I've been talking to C.B. Too much.

   Which means I'm either going nutburger or I'm lonely as hell. Either way, it's not good.

2. Cardboard Ben is not helping me with my novel.

   I thought having him around would help inspire me to nurture my own artistic greatness. But I think I find him intimidating. In fact, my novel, my third attempt at a novel, is painfully awful. I am considering shredding it and using it in one of my collages.

3. C.B. is not making me feel any better about Roger.

And he is not helping me overcome my anxiety or my need to drink wine, smoke pot, and play bad guitar. He is a god-damn cardboard smaller-than-life man.

4. Max peed on C.B.

I think. C.B.'s left leg and foot are sort of warped and stained. It smells like pee. Yeah, it does.

"Character motivation," Nikki said. "What is it?"

"Why the character does what she does," Willow said.

"Good, Willow. In a story or novel, the characters want things. The tension happens when the characters don't get those things."

"Like how you want Ben Stevens the rock star."

Nikki shook her head. "Okay everyone, listen. I don't want Ben Stevens. I just think it's interesting that he's famous."

"We don't know him," Karen said.

"I know," Nikki said. "And I know we're getting off topic here, don't think I don't know that, but here's the stupid thing I did. I took this smaller-than-lifesize cardboard cutout of Ben from the record store. Well, actually, Trevor let me take it. And it stands in my living room."

"Why did you do that?" Cody asked.

"Good question."

"Well, what was your motivation Miss West?" Karen said.

"I don't know. Sometimes I think people do things and they aren't really sure why. I think it was because I thought maybe he'd help me feel like I could be better than I am. Or maybe it was total whim. And I knew him so I thought it would be cool. I really don't know."

"I think you're really cool, Miss West," Victor said.

"Yeah, me too," Willow said.

"Don't be such loser suckups," Jake said.

"Gee, thanks, Jake," Nikki said. "Everyone finish chapter eight for Friday."

Nikki read at stoplights. It was a bad habit and led to cars beeping. Today she heard shouts. "Miss West! Miss West!" She looked to the right and there was a big yellow school bus, her kids leaning out the windows, shouting and waving and smiling.

Their teacher, in her car, after school!

She smiled at their excitement and waved back.

Driving home, she sang with the radio, off-key, loud. No matter.

"Sorry, Cardboard Ben," Nikki said.

She held him like a surfboard under her arm. It was dark. Her neighbor had not left the porch light on.

"It wasn't really working, C.B.," she continued. "It was just something I did, taking you. It doesn't make sense, you know."

She put him down, pushed his feet into the ground some.

"Keep playing your music," she said and patted his shoulder. "Nice to see you again."

She walked back to her house, leaving Cardboard Ben Stevens standing on her neighbor's lawn, right next to the orange-haired dancing sculpture. Nikki figured he'd be good there until the summer rains.

Making the Bed

Poetry

I walk into the bedroom and for some reason, perhaps it is the soft gray of rainy light in lines across the bed, I consider the form of poetry typically done in middle school, the concrete poem in which descriptive words are used to outline the shape of the thing itself: *mattress mattress mattress* in a large rectangle and *pillow pillow pillow pillow* in squares.

Today, were I to write a concrete poem, though I am thirty-two and write free verse and ad copy, and on good days, recipe cards for friends, if I did write a concrete poem, it would include my random mix of poorly scripted caps and lowercase: the words *goose-down mattress, linen throw pillows, green sheets,* and I would sketch a small dog named *Brodie* who sleeps on your side of the bed, his little body a ray of black fur.

I would not use a ruler. Life is not about straight lines, crisp edges. *Tangledsheetstangledsheetstangledsheets.*

Concrete poem, haiku, pantoum. Words will not make the bed.

Mother's Words

Or maybe they will.

"Make your bed, Deborah."

"But why?"

"Because I said so."

Make the bed.

It never made sense when I was younger, my mother's need for *my* bed to be made. But now it does. There is wisdom in "You'll understand when you're older." There is wisdom in "Because I said so."

Because there is something to be said for tired legs sliding into smoothed sheets, tucked corners.

It is true. The cacophonous romp of morning sheets is not the same as the quiet haven of evening's made bed.

Thread Count

We hadn't gotten new sheets since the wedding, when we didn't know anything about thread counts. We looked at colors and pricing and thought about how a wedding registry was something weird. Plateware and flatware and sheets. What did we know?

We were getting married. It had nothing to do with setting up house, with obtaining the right appliances, the right necessities, things that had not seemed necessary before.

So maybe they are not the finest sheets, but they are worn and washed and stained in the right way, darker where our bodies lie night after night, and someone might say those are love spots and I'd say they were right.

Two sets. Light blue. Mint green. Two hundred thread count. Ocean colors. Waves of sheets. Sometimes I mix and match the wedding sheets with this new set I recently bought on sale. Dark blue. Egyptian cotton. Higher thread count.

Perhaps they are softer, the dark blue sheets. Perhaps the night my head sleeps on a dark blue pillow, I dream sweeter. Perhaps with the Egyptian cotton I dream of sandstorms and ancient pleasures, of lapis and chalcedony, cool stones rubbed along meridians.

It is something to consider, since they are the sheets I hold in my hands.

Stripping

Sometimes you say "Strip for me," and I do, with a seriousness that is comical. You like that I hum a stripping song, the same tune every time. Sometimes there is real music already playing, something bluesy and wailing and it makes it all easier, the slow removal of items, the revelation that we are body, when it all comes down to it, we are body.

But today it is the bed to be stripped. Fresh sheets. No music.

Quilting

We have a patchwork quilt. It is not my grandmother's nor is it made by a great aunt. There is not a story in the denim square, the daisied corner. It is not a matriarch's apron swatch that sits dead center. It is just a patchwork quilt, store-bought, to make our home feel country-like, to make me believe that even though outside are sidewalks and carports and well-kept lawns and kids on bikes, inside are long fields and wildflowers and mountain air and river water.

Pillows

We each use two pillows. You sleep with yours under your head. I hug my second pillow, curve it into my body as if it is a child. I often wake and find it on the floor.

Leo is Coming

Yes, I remember what it was like, yes, you coming home and how I'd be there, lying atop a made bed, waiting, and yes back then there were no fantasies, there was just us and yes it was good enough. There were no ghosts, no phantoms to rattle chains and knock bedposts and make us wake from sleep.

Yes.

I remember.

Other Beds

Sleeping under the dining room table and saying it was a cave; camp bunk beds and sandy feet; beds in college with revolving boys; hotel beds with starchy sheets; and beds I do not speak of, beds that are embedded—ha—in memory, and need not be told.

Bedtime Stories

Why does the tenderness come when you are gone? Why is it that absence, the stillness of house, the expansiveness of bed, is something that makes me miss you? And why then, when I hear your hand on the doorknob, when I hear the scuff of your shoes on the floor, do I suddenly wish I could fall back on the bed, that it would fly up and out the window, a magic carpet from an *Arabian Nights* tale, that somehow I'd leave it all behind. I'd wave goodbye, and you'd wave back, and it would all be okay for that to happen. For me to take off for awhile. It would all be okay.

Take

Frannie Bernstein saw the pack of gum in her daughter's small fist on the drive home from the grocery store. The ice cream would melt if she said anything, if they turned around and drove the miles back to the store, but Frannie had to say something.

"Stella Scarlet Bernstein, where did you get that pack of gum?" Frannie asked her daughter, who was sitting there kicking her legs, tapping her fingers on her little blue jeans while she sang along with The Beatles.

Frannie wondered if it was this, listening to *Abbey Road*, all silky wavery warble and eye-flutter fantastic rather than something more simple like *A Hard Day's Night*, that was setting her child to thieving. She laughed, she didn't mean to, but the brief thought was so ridiculous, and then Stella laughed too, because sometimes she was a perfect mimic of her mother. Frannie had to frown because Stella needed to know that things weren't right.

"Did you take that gum from the store?" Frannie asked. "You took that gum, Stella. That's not right."

Frannie looked for the next possible turn so she could head back to the store, but then she just slowed down, tried to make a smooth transition—movement and then a stopping—and pulled off to the side of the road, put the car in park.

Precious little Stella Scarlet, all four years of her, with her striped mitten—they hadn't found the other mitten, it was somewhere, lost in a scuffle of toys and shoes and coloring book pages—so that the other small hand was bare, the one that had been holding the gum, but now the gum was gone. Hidden. Or, Frannie wondered, was it just some hallucination, some momentary vision, like when she saw gray movements in corners or the ferns in the front yard unfurling while she pulled weeds?

She turned the music off.

"Where's the gum?" Frannie asked, and then there was a honking, a hooting, and a truckload of baseball caps, bare-handed waves and words on wind.

Stella looked down at her mittened hand, traced the stripes. She didn't look up at her mother.

Stella, sweet love child. Sweet girl conceived during a night of Grateful Dead and diamond pinpoints in the sky, a blanket in an open field, moist lips and hip thrusts toward moonlight, Frannie's arms wrapped around Reuben's skinny hippie-man body, their minds exploding with color and kaleidoscope and their bodies so ridiculous and weighty, the night air cool and their skin both hot and cold, and then, later, a velvet shade descending, submerging them into sleep. Trip out, trip in, morning comes and not then, only weeks later, knowledge of Stella, baby coming, baby baby, rock-a-by, rock-n-roll.

"Stella," Frannie said. "Look at me."

Stella looked up and her brown eyes were tearing. She put her pink-tipped fingers to her eyes. An actress, my daughter the actress, Frannie thought. She is me.

Stella, sweet love child, conceived by accident, created in Leary-dipped moonlight, a reason to marry Reuben, though maybe it would have happened anyway, two years together, and really, at twenty-five, why not get married, especially with a baby coming.

"Sweetie," Frannie said. "What did you do with the gum?" The sweetie came without thought, it was an endearment at a wrong time, a time of lesson, right and wrong, but here, her daughter crying, lost in that moment of confession and consequence.

"Stella. You're not supposed to take things. You know this, yes?"

Not like Frannie, with a brief history of thieving.

And hopefully this wasn't the start of lying, because that could last forever, like how Frannie told Reuben nothing was wrong, even when she was sitting in the rocker on the porch, considering taking Stella, moving back to Florida where it was warm and sunny and the beach a year-round occasion. She wasn't a northern girl, and here she was, winter weary and mother of a one-mitten girl parked on a road in upstate New York. All because Reuben had gotten his addled head together, decided a Ph.D. in English was what he needed. Who cared that Frannie had a fine job, a good deal working as the head manager at a health-food store? That didn't matter; they packed up and headed north. So when Reuben asked, "What's wrong?" she lied and said, "Nothing."

"Taking things you haven't paid for—things that aren't yours—is bad, Stella."

"Yes."

"And lying about it is bad too."

And then Stella was really crying, her face scrunched, tears, tears—where did all the tears come from? Stella was a good child, a quiet child, and yet today, a moment of deviousness, a taking, a hiding, a sobbing.

Kind of like Frannie's own childhood deviousness, a button stuck in the nose, just a thing to do, until her mother, who had been sewing said, "Where's that button that was here on the table, Francine?" and Frannie mumbling, "I don't know," even though the button was in her nose, shoved up there quietly, it hurt, kind of, she wanted it out. Finally she had to say, "Mommy, the button is in my nose," forced higher by probing fingers, until they had to go to the doctor who said it would come out, a good sneeze, a good blowing, and yes, the button did come out later that night.

The gum was not in Stella's nose. It was squashed under her leg.

"Stella…"

"I'm sorry, Mommy."

Sorry. Such a good word. What did it mean really?

She said sorry when she got too moody, when she cried about how things weren't what she expected, and Reuben said sorry when he came home late and when he came home a little drunk because some folks went and got beers after an exam, and sorry was just a word, sometimes.

"And you know," she said aloud. "Some people don't even say sorry. They just start taking things. First it's a pack of gum, then earrings, then a pair of shoes, and it doesn't stop. Then it's someone's husband, and what was she thinking really, little hussy grad student, didn't she know he had a wife and a daughter at home? Did she think she could just take him?"

"Yes."

"Yes?" Frannie looked at Stella, who was nodding, her mouth a serious pout. "Stella?"

"Mommy?"

Frannie glanced at the gas tank. It was dangerously low. When did that happen? The gas tank on empty and her wallet with only a dollar or two, and things like this happened it seemed. She could turn around, get gas, take Stella back to the grocery, but she didn't have the money to get the gas, and she could probably make it home with what was left in the tank, or she could use the credit card, but then her husband would know, and he'd want to know why she was using the credit card. And how could she tell him she had used the cash for a massage, a facial, she had given herself a spa day—something luxurious and ridiculous—and she had loved it, simply loved it, though it was a secret.

"Mommy..."

"Yes, Stella." She looked at her daughter, felt the pinch at the back of her neck, a kink again, the spa day down the drain.

"I'm sorry," Stella said, and Frannie had a feeling Stella was saying sorry, not about the gum, but because Frannie was crying, Frannie was crying and she only then realized it.

It was Reuben's fault really. Because if he hadn't been so involved in school, if he had considered Stella, Frannie, if he had thought about spending some time with them and not with the other students, not with that girl named Cheryl, well then maybe Frannie wouldn't hate the north so much.

Stella was pulling off her mitten, tugging at her fingers.

"Just say okay," Frannie said. "Just tell me okay."

"Okay," Stella said. "Okay."

"Don't lie, don't cheat, don't steal," Frannie said. "These are things that mess you up. You wake in the morning and you feel awful. You mess things up. And sometimes it's because you don't know what else to do, and sometimes it's because you have nowhere to hide. The mind comes with you, honey, always."

Frannie picked her daughter's mitten off the car seat. It was small, so small, she marveled that her daughter's hand fit it.

"Say okay," she said. Stella was staring straight ahead, her eyes blinking, like she was trying to process the information, add it all up, or maybe she was trying to stop new tears.

"Okay."

"Good."

"Mommy," Stella said. "I have to pee."

"We'll be home soon, sweetie. Can you hold it?"

Stella bit her lip, her little teeth pressing pink to white. "I think so."

"That's good. We'll go."

And when Frannie pulled back onto the road, she thought she'd just drive home, she'd let her daughter pee, she'd put the ice cream in the freezer, and then maybe tomorrow they'd take the gum back. Enough lessons for today.

"Tomorrow we'll take the gum back."

"Tomorrow we go skating," Stella said.

"Yes, that too."

Frannie pressed the power button on the stereo. She was listening to Stella bang-bang with "Maxwell's Silver Hammer" and driving fast to make it home before the gas ran out when she saw the red and blue lights in her rear view mirror, and she thought about gunning it, just making an escape, mother and child at top speed—it could be the kind of resolution needed. But instead she slowed, and for a moment she closed her eyes, let the lights become something lovely from the past, like lights from the psychedelic cosmos, lights from an easy time from forever ago, and Frannie reached for Stella's bare hand. She had no idea about mothering, she had no idea, but some things you couldn't take back, some things stayed with you.

Young Woman Seated in the Art Museum

Hallway walls of glass let in the afternoon sky, which is gray and ominous with storm clouds. The floor is slick wood, light grain oak, shiny like an ice pond, but not like an ice pond. White. Everything is white. White walls, white benches, white lights above. White and light wood and glass and gray clouds. Voices echo, footsteps echo, perhaps the scratch of my pen echoes. Let me write quickly and listen. Echo? Yes. Echo.

The security guard at his desk, has he read the brochure on this new pavilion *dedicated to showcasing contemporary art*? Does he read behind his desk—

something pre-approved like *ARTnews* or *The New Yorker*? Or does he read the sports page? A mystery novel? Does he wish he could pull a piece of gum from his pocket, for mint-fresh breath in case a lovely, lonely woman wants to know where the Lichtenstein is?

It is so quiet. Just me. The guard. Nobody else.

Will he allow me the freedom to do what I wish? *Experiments in art.* Will he let me sing loud, very loud, an opera, an aria, something made-up, but believable, words like dolce vita, vibrato, my voice building and rising to meet ceiling, to catch within Calder's mobile, *painted sheet metal and wire*, to bounce from white walls, from glass, so that the freestanding sculptures might respond, so that, perhaps, the bronze variation on the Venus de Milo might drop to her knees? I might say applaud, but she is armless.

Will the guard call for backup? Or will he continue to draw small spirals on his lunch napkin while I pull a pair of roller skates from my satchel, while I lace and then race, skate on these fabulous wood floors, my hands almost—but not—brushing the walls, the multi-media works, *chrome and wood and fiber*, the Abstract Expressionist paintings with their *intensely emotional and independent spirit.* Will he yell, "All skate, in the opposite direction!" and give me a silent thumbs-up as I whirl, maneuver, find myself skating where I have already been?

Maybe, just maybe, he will help me set up a small display in a corner, on the floor, a colorful shawl, silk patterned and playful, spread out on the ground so I might show my own work, sketches I've done on a notepad of the man I once loved. I have destroyed many. I have saved some. *Reconfigured materials.*

Does the guard with his uniform and his serious stare long for me? For someone to create something *introspective and expressive* in this still-life of a museum? A giggle, it escapes me. It echoes, tumbles, and rolls alongside Venus' legs. It slides along a series of photographs. A giggle, a misplaced *blurring of boundaries*; he is watching me, frowning. I must rise now. Go. Skate.

Luckily, Lucy Sims Has No Stamps

Dear Bed Bath & Beyond:

I am writing to request a discount on twin size sheets. Specifically, white and beige—and a couple of black. I'd like to purchase a dozen of these sheets. Not sets. No pillowcases or fitted sheets. Just regular ones.

You may wonder why I need a dozen. I don't run a summer camp and I don't have a large family. I don't have a family at all. I need the sheets for myself. I'll be blunt. I'm tired of the fashion industry. I'm tired of shopping only to find that clothes I once thought were just right are on super-reduced clearance because they're old and outdated. I'm tired of buying a nice shirt just to find that I have no pants or skirt to go with it. I'm tired of the constant battle with weight gain and loss, which makes my jeans either pinch or cinch or sag. Really, I'm just tired.

I'm starting my own trend. Tunics. Roman togas. Greek chitons. Back to the heady ancient days. Sure, people will think I'm crazy at first. Aren't all true visionaries considered mad? But really, a well draped sheet—it's nice. Full of flow and simplicity. A single strand of pearls, an opal drop pendant—I'll be stunning. Black sheets will be reserved for evening wear, for when I start dating again, which hopefully will be soon. The whites and beiges are for daytime. I'm trying to keep it simple, and really, the elegance of white or beige cannot be denied.

Yes, there will be those who mock me, who will laugh and say, "Can't get your sheet together, can you?" and there will be those who will tell me a windbreaker over a tunic is a faux pas, but I say to Hades with them. I'll be comfortable and satisfied. I'll have extra hours, those hours I spent in stores looking through racks and racks of clothes, and with those hours I can sew and knit and paint and maybe even find an algorithm for world peace.

I have to say, I got the idea from a Greek-Roman Festival we recently held at my school. To get kids enthusiastic—which believe me, can sometimes be hard—I wore a chiton the whole week before the festival. I said I was Athena, but really I'm no warrior goddess. I suppose I'm no Aphrodite either, though wasn't it Keats—or Shelley?—who said while looking at a Grecian urn, "Beauty is truth, truth beauty."

Now what does that mean? Sometimes the truth is really not beautiful at all.

You know, come to think of it, maybe I could help you out. I could bring some students in one day and we could wear our sheets and roam the aisles and pass out olives. Use some of those specialty toothpicks you sell. Or hand out baklava on a nice serving dish. Then we could point people toward kitchenwares and mention a sale on bed linens too.

Quid pro quo. Sheets for a great sales gimmick.

All I ask is that you consider my request for a thirty-five percent discount on a dozen sheets. Five white, five beige, two black. The nice Egyptian cotton ones.

Best,
Lucy Sims

Dear Mrs. Duncan:

You won't remember me. Or at least I hope not, since I was pretty pathetic in seventh grade. I was the girl with the really bad haircut and the oversized glasses that sat next to Melissa Richter, who one day lit a cigarette in your class and took two puffs before she put it out on the heel of her navy blue espadrille, and when you walked by you said, "Bad habit to start," and Melissa rolled her eyes, and I stared straight ahead at the chalkboard because I was scared as hell of Melissa and her friends. They were just mean and stupid. I was just smart and ugly.

Anyway, I'm writing because I've had a glass of wine—okay, two—and I want to ask for forgiveness. While you were busy trying to teach us about Steinbeck's desire to write about the poor and downtrodden, I was making sketches in my notebook of your flyaway hair and crooked teeth. And one night, my best friend Hillary Swanson and I called your house and sang in really bad falsetto voices like we were opera stars. We called about four times in one night. We laughed so hard we almost peed in our pants, but we didn't like you much and thought you were the worst teacher ever. Back then we didn't understand teachers, and I hate to think I was so foolish and wicked. Maybe you were trying to watch a movie with your husband that night. Maybe you were trying to teach your child to read, or maybe you were just sitting writing a letter to your mother, and we kept calling and singing in really bad voices until we giggled too much and had to hang up.

This was before caller ID. If kids called and sang bad opera today, they'd be busted. *Carmen, Madame Butterfly, Babes in Toyland.* I tell you those kids would be in trouble.

Maybe you still are an English teacher, and if so, good for you. It is a noble profession. I'm a teacher now too. Social Studies. Actually I don't remember all that much from your class, except a couple things like the Melissa Richter incident and also the day you got your period and it made a red dot on your pants and then we secretly called you Red Dot for the rest of the year.

How shameful, really. I hope you can accept my apology. And if you can remember what song we were singing, because for some reason I can't, will you please let me know? It's been bugging me, and Hillary Swanson and I don't talk anymore, on account that she went and got famous and beautiful.

Also, even if you don't remember the song, do you remember the way you got us to remember the difference between lay and lie? I always forget that.

Sincerely,
Lucy (Mavis) Sims

Dear Bill:

While I was unpacking boxes, I found one of your Speedos. The dark blue banana hammock one. Now that I can say it without hurting your "sensitive side," let me just say this: I prefer a man in surf shorts. I'm enclosing the suit. It's really incredible that your hairy ass can even fit in this thing. Glad you won't be around my pool.

Lu

Dear Primo Italiano Café Manager (I think your name is Bernardo):

I am a loyal customer. You know me, my voice, I call a couple times a week, and even come in sometimes for dinner on Tuesdays, when you have your Spaghetti Slam Special. I'm the thirty-something woman with the red curls. Recently I cut my hair, and your delivery boy with the missing front tooth told me it looked good, which was nice because I think I look like Ronald McDonald now.

I'm writing because often when I call, I get put on hold. It's fine, I understand that lots of people are calling for delivery. But what I want to say may take some explaining.

You have a great delivery service. You're fast and efficient and have never gotten my order wrong, unlike the Chinese place next door to you—those guys once gave me cashew beef instead of chicken and I absolutely do not eat beef. Chicken is fine. Fish too. In fact, fish is what I want to ask about. On the other side of the Chinese place is a nice little sushi place. I particularly like the salmon roll and the spicy tuna roll. But they don't deliver. What if you set up a delivery partnership with them? Would that be possible? I get these sushi cravings, which may have something to do with protein deficiency or iron deficiency since I drink a lot of coffee and I skip breakfast most days. Anyway, I know it would be ridiculous of me to ask you to start serving sushi—you guys don't have the space for a sushi bar, unless you get rid of that big family-sized table—so I thought I'd suggest a sushi delivery program for loyal customers like me. The place is called New Sushi. Nice folks there.

I suppose I should also mention that I've got a new address. I'm still in your delivery range—I know because I called and asked just yesterday, right before I had to go lay down (or is it lie?) because lately I'm just so tired, which is why I have to order food for delivery so often. Well, that and the fact that I'm lacking in basic kitchen appliances.

Let me know what you decide so I can call over to New Sushi and give them a heads up. And tell your toothless delivery boy that he really made me feel better about myself.

Gratzi-nara (Get it? An Italian-Japanese combo for thank you and goodbye),
Lucy
224-C West Magnolia

Dear Parents:

Well it's that time of year again. Semester grades are due for your children. I'll be brief, since I know you are busy. I'm busy too. I've got papers I haven't graded that are two months old, and just the other morning the cat knocked my coffee cup over and it spilled on a stack of essay tests that your children just took. Nice timing, actually—if I had to read another word on the American system of checks and balances I'd tear my hair out.

All this, and my recent divorce. It hasn't left me in the mood for teaching, really. I mean, how am I to impart wisdom about the Bill of Rights when Bill, my ex, is just a Bill of Wrongs. Ha. Bad joke. But can you blame me? I'm hurting. Sometimes I'll stop in the middle of a lesson and just talk to the kids about life. My life, really. Maybe they've shared this with you, though maybe not, because when you ask most kids what they did in school, they reply, "Nothing." In this case, they may be right. My deepest apologies. Also, I may have said Asswipe in class once or twice.

And now, I've just moved into a new place. Smaller, but closer to the school. I may even start biking to work, though I'm worried that my new tunic dress will get caught in the spokes.

Anyhow, here's what I propose. I need things, and so I'm selling grades.

To buy your child an A, I'd like one of the following: a microwave, a toaster oven, a blender, an espresso maker, mixing bowls and a nice set of baking pans, or a portable CD player. But please, talk to other parents before purchasing. I don't want duplicates.

For a B, I'd like bath towels, preferably in sea colors, a set of cloth napkins, wine glasses, maybe a vase or two. The apartment complex has a nice pool area, so I could also use some pool towels. Please don't consider buying me swimwear—you know how tricky bathing suit shopping can be. Maybe a gift certificate to one of the department stores.

For a C, I'll take a plant. Orchids are lovely. Some people say they're too hard to nurture, but I take care of children all day. Surely I can take care of plants.

I also like gerber daisies and violets.

To buy your child a D, please send some stationery. I'm running out of good paper. Matching envelopes would be nice too.

And finally, F's are free. Really.

Talk it over with your child and let me know before next Friday, when grades are due. And please, don't hesitate to contact me if you have any other offers. I'm open to suggestions.

I'm glad in this day and age we can continue to have parents and teachers working together.

Best,
Lucinda Sims
Social Studies, Barton Middle School

Dear Bill:

Me again. I'm requesting that you send those "artful pictures" you took of me years ago in that hotel in Cancun. I had several tequila shots and you told me I looked model-like. Remember? During our happy days.

I should also tell you I went to Harrison's Pawn Shop and sold my engagement ring. And your saxophone. I figured you hadn't played it in a long time and surely you don't have time now that you've got that new girlfriend. I know the sax was your Grandpa Nick's and he played with Tito Puente once, but it's your style to give up older things to get newer stuff, so I thought surely you wouldn't have a problem.

Anyway, while I was at the pawn shop, I bought myself a left-handed electric guitar and an amp.

Rock on,

Cinda

Live at the Palace Theatre

May 16—Doors Open at 8

Dear Mrs. Sims:

I've had some wine this evening and I'm feeling sort of honest.

Funny that I never did call you Mother. Or Ma. You kind of look like a Ma, with that apron and those sensible shoes. But it's probably well enough. I mean, what kind of a mother-in-law would let her future daughter marry such a complete idiot? A hint or two, right before the wedding would have been enough. You could have pointed at any attractive woman in the pews, and made some crazy complicated thrusting motions, some weird corkscrew gyrations, just like Bill does during sex. I would have understood. I would have pulled off the veil, flung the garter and headed home.

Some kind of mother-in-law.

I'm writing to ask about your Poppy Seed Baklava. Would you mind sending the recipe? I have a copy somewhere in Bill's house but when I asked him to mail it he told me there was no recipe file. But we know he lies. And lays. I'd stop over to take a look myself, but that little harlot, that teaching assistant, might be there. And I am just not ready for that. I wonder if she's seen Bill in a Speedo yet? That might *teach* her a thing or two.

Well, Mrs. Sims, I need to get going. I'm tired. I've got a guitar lesson tomorrow and some practicing to do—practicing for a new life. So please do send along that recipe. I'd like to try some baking once I get new pans and a mixing bowl set at the end of this semester.

Moving on,
Lucy

Blush

Little white Keds, not so white, not as sweet and stiff as when they were just bought and nestled in the slim shoebox, little blue rubber label on the heel so obvious and so perfectly new, those speckled white sneakers are tossed in the backseat of an old Toyota, tossed atop a Biology book and a tennis racket and some canned goods for the homeroom food drive—green beans and kidney beans and oh man, oh man, waxed beans with their yellow alien skin—those sneakers, so childish, so innocent, so easygoing, are put aside so she can slip her feet into something more grown up.

Pale pink pumps. Blush cheek, innocent and naughty those pumps, her feet slide, her calves arch, not that anyone could see with her legs in jeans, but ah, there, the lift, the heightening, the womanliness of such a shoe.

Click click clickity clack she walks from the car to the convenience store, those pumps like adrenaline, like bravery stamped upon her feet. She saunters, sashays, her woman hips blooming, she is in her favorite blue button down blouse and her jeans that make her look as thin as she can be, thin she is not, and she staccatos across the parking lot, gives a nod to the other kids from her high school who hunch down in car seats rolling joints, sit cross-legged on the hoods of cars counting cash, she moves into the light, the fluorescent lights, the neon Budweiser and Kool signs, she steps and tiptotters, graceful, purposeful, she says to herself. Old enough. Old enough, she repeats, and she tries not to bite her lipsticked lips. Sunrise Glimmer. Palest pink to match the shoes.

He doesn't say hello. He doesn't even look up, the man at the counter, there every Friday night, when the high school kids come in and buy chips and pretzels to indulge marijuana munchies, they buy bean dip, big sodas to pour whiskey in, licorice, the guys buy ham and Swiss sandwiches or hot dogs on a dare, the girls buy mint gum, and some kids with fake IDs buy cheap strawberry and peach screwtop wine. The man behind the counter with his thin mustache and his grayed-out front tooth watches a little television and palms a baseball in his hand. He doesn't care that Alice comes walking in, her pale pink lips turning slightly blue in the fluorescent lights. He shouts at the TV and hisses at the air and ignores the tiptap tiptap of heels across the store floor.

"Hey Alice," she hears, and she scowls, shakes her head at Laura Alvarez who is standing looking at chocolate bars. Alice shakes her head because she isn't Alice right now, no, no, no, she is Dana Kay Nichelson, age 21, born May 10, a Taurus, and ask, ask the address and Alice will rattle it back to you, 16 West Harper Drive.

Alice taptaptaps past the chocolate bars and past the party-size bags of potato chips, past the rotating hotdogs and dank coffee pots, and opens the refrigerated section, finds the bottle of wine, pauses, bites her lip in what she hopes is a real way. Then she walks, confidently, step one and two, Dana Kay Nichelson up to the counter where finally the cashier notices her.

"ID?" he says, and Alice smiles, reaches into the back pocket of her jeans, her heart beating bumbumbum, and she remembers how her father explained the sound is more like lubdublubdub, and she thinks, that doesn't matter now, bumbum or lubdub, it's her heart beating fast as she pulls the ID she recently got from her older sister's friend out of the back pocket of her jeans.

Alice thinks curly hair, big curly hair, long crazy red-brown corkscrew curls, grow, grow, grow. She resists the urge to fluff it one more time, her own curls not as wild, not actually corkscrewy, more viney. "Beautiful hair" is what everyone says, and this makes up for her thick athletic legs and her average face. What they can't say, not to her average face, is "big breasts," which is true, so they say, "beautiful hair," which is also true. She resists the urge to fluff, she keeps her hands at her sides while Mr. Baseball looks at her ID. She thinks dimple, left cheek, she smiles trying to make her brown eyes squint up like Dana Kay Nichelson, and she tries to stand tall in her heels, Dana Kay 5'7", although Alice is only 5'2". All this mimicry, and Mr. Graytooth doesn't even look at her, not really, he glances up and down, and then he looks past Alice, frowns, and her palms go cold at her sides. Clench, unclench. The clerk yells, "Chips buy one get one free!" and his breath is strong of peppermint, surprisingly fresh and clean, this puff of mint, "Buy one get one free!" and then he punches register keys with his left hand. In his right hand, he holds the baseball down against the counter, his fingers wrapped like an eagle's claw and Alice can see the baseball is scuffed with blue and black marks, a long line of green too.

"Wine not free," Graytooth says and Alice blushes, Dana Kay blushes, and then he yells, "I'm watching you!" and Alice realizes he's not talking to her but to the noisy guys at the back of the store, one of whom is singing the Allman Brother's *Midnight Rider* in a pretty good voice. She doesn't want to turn around and see what's going on, so she slides her money across the counter, hooks her free hand into the front pocket of her jeans—studied, casual waiting.

Graytooth takes the money, his long fingers plucking the bill, and Alice grins, foolish grin on her face, a smile plastered, she understands this, a smile plastered because there it is, stuck, this grin, so much so that she has to force herself to let it dip slightly, to realign into nonchalance, into this means nothing, nothing at all, even while her friends sit in the car watching, waiting, and right now they are most likely grinning too, plastered grins, and maybe Sadie is pulling the weed out of the little wooden traveling box her brother gave her before he left for college, and maybe Claudine is blowing bubbles with her gum because that's what she does—blows bubbles and thickens her eyeliner—and Alice is about to reach for the wine bottle when Graytooth says, "Move!"

Alice freezes. Move? She can hear the hum of the television on the counter, she hears the crack of the baseball bat, she hears the low voice of the radio, also on, somewhere under the counter, Spanish news, maybe—the deep crackly voice has the monotone of newscast. She hears the blur of sound, she hears "Move" but she can't move. Not fast enough.

"Move," he says again and he motions her to the side and then she does. She bobbles a bit on her pump, rolls her ankle, ouch, a sharp pain shoots up her calf, and then Graytooth throws the baseball across the store, smack, it hits the wall, and Alice turns to see three guys standing at the back. Frozen boys. Eyebrows raised, hands raised. Palmer Monroe and his buddies Kenny and Stretch. Baseball players.

"I could have hit you!" Graytooth shouts. "Get out!"

The three guys move fast, scuttle, bumble, almost a cavort, a shuffle dance, toward the door. Palmer smiles at Alice and then he is gone.

Alice watches wide-eyed, but then her mouth moves involuntarily into smile.

"Not funny," Graytooth says to her. He rubs his shoulder, a scowl on his face. "Thieves."

"I…" she starts but then the clerk motions with his hand. "Get that for me," he says. He motions toward the baseball, which is in front of a display of Pepsi cans.

Alice hesitates, looks to Graytooth, whose hand is now on the wine bottle. She heads for the baseball. She's hurt her ankle; she can feel how it twinges when she walks and so she tiptaps slowly, carefully.

Damn pumps, she thinks. She is not a girl-of-pumps. She is a shuffshuff sneakers girl, a flipflop girl, flipflop flipflop. She is not like some of the girls who wear pumps and high wedges to school, who clickity clack and swish in tight jeans up to he's-cute-for-a-teacher Mr. Coffey's desk—"Well how do we know when the two trains will meet? I just don't get it."—so that poor Mr.Coffey, his wife so very ugly, that awful dress she wears so loose and floral in the picture he has taped to the upper corner of the chalkboard, poor Mr. Coffey, he coughs and picks at his fingernails and later the students see him smoking in the teacher's parking lot and staring up at the sky.

The ball is warm when she hands it back. Graytooth palms the baseball and holds it up like an offering.

"Could have been in the pros," Graytooth says. "Threw my shoulder out. Ruined my game."

Alice nods. Crackle. Roar. Crowd cheer.

"Ruined my game," he repeats. He gives her the change. "Too soon."

Alice takes the wine bottle and smiles her own Alice smile, and tiptap tiptap she limps slightly, slowly toward the door.

Outside, Alice stumbles, hobbles. Her whispered string of "shits" and "god-damns" hit the parking lot pavement before her, and she is almost at her car, she can see the girls giving her the thumbs up, when she realizes she forgot the ID. Dana Kay Nichelson left there at the register. Alice turns to head back, her ankle rolls, rolls again, and the wine bottle slips, falls, shattered glass, splattered pumps, pink pumps. Blush. She bends down carefully, tottering on one foot, she pulls off one pump, then the other. Shoes in one hand, she looks to the One Stop and can see Graytooth is watching his television, one hand cupping his shoulder. She thinks she sees his lips moving as if he were reciting a prayer, or a curse. The glass is in chunks, big, small, around her. She stares at her pale white feet against the asphalt and waits for someone to tell her what to do next.

The Guitar Case

His guitar case is old, edges scuffed and smoothed, seams frayed, picked up, put down, banged in the back of vans and against hardwood floors, plunked upon cheap Persian rugs, and the case is stickered, bands and bands and slogans and grooved-out graphics, and got to love a peace-lovin' man, a guy who can say I love you to anyone, because he does, he loves the idea of you, a guy like that, with baggy jeans slung low, feet sandaled and his hair a mess of wild curls, a glint, truly a glint in his eye, his bearded cheek all wise and wicked, a guy like that, whose fingers brush guitar strings and coax, tease music, a guy like that, his velvet-lined guitar case open there on the side of the bar's tiny stage, well a guy like that makes me wish I could curl myself up, fit myself inside that case, so that later, when the set is done, when he's looked over the audience with a small bite of his lip and shake of his head, when he's ready to go home and sleep the sleep of angels and rock stars, I'll be there, and I'll say, "There's not room in here for me and that guitar," and then he'll pull me out and play my chords, ones I didn't know I had.

Dewey Classifies Love

000 GENERALITIES

When Sage Leary, one of those heavenly drifting boys, with backpack torn and frayed in that romantic way of intellectuals and idealists, drifts out of Daphne's life, it is not a quiet moment.

There are drums pounding, guitars shrieking, wailing, gypsies rotating, gyrating, arms up above, hips swiveling and snaking, finger cymbals clickety-clackety ting-ting-ting. The sky rips colors apart, bands of orange, grey, pink, blue, dissipating, dropping into darkness.

Later, she will spill her wineglass. It tumbles and rolls, makes its way under the cocktail table, and there—when Daphne bends down to retrieve it—she finds an encyclopedia, volume S, Sage has left for her to return to the library. Daphne the librarian sits back on the couch, leafing through pages.

"It's one year," he had said to her. "An experience," he said when he told her he was going to teach English in Spain.

"I'll be back," he said. She needs to believe him.

100 PHILOSOPHY & PSYCHOLOGY

Sage Leary's departure.

It is not really like this, with drums and gypsies, but this is how Daphne would describe it. It is, truthfully, more like this: a clock ticking in the hallway, the hum of an old refrigerator, the creaks and cricks and cracks of wood floors expanding, shifting, settling, the small symphony of a house.

And then there is a door closing, a woman falling onto the couch, eyes closed, breath forced into her fingers as she presses and pulls at her lips, trying to imprint what she believes is a last kiss.

Yes, it is more like that.

But emotion colors perception.

Daphne looks around the living room. The sky has darkened, sending grey and blue shadows through the blinds, crisscrossing the table, her legs, the wine glass, the opened book.

She must rise, move toward the bedroom, where

she hopes to sleep, to dream, to wake and find it is all dream.

200 RELIGION

"I am nothing like my namesake, like Daphne of the river," she says into the mirror. She wipes her face with a hand towel; she stops, peers at herself. She is a small woman, her dark curls too long, her lips too thin. She is not the sort of woman a man like Sage would want. But here she is with his promise: "I will return."

He had sat in the library day after day, working on translations of poetry, Spanish to English, trying to capture the cadence of language. He had pursued her; she had laughed, thought it unlikely the long-haired, bearded boy should want her, the shy bookish woman.

Daphne, the daughter of a river god, rejected the god Apollo. Who could reject a god, a man of power and strength, a man of the sun, rays of heat, warmth, growth? Daphne, the daughter of a mechanical engineer, tried—really she did—until she could no longer evade him.

In the mythology, Daphne asks for help and is turned into a laurel tree. Daphne the librarian did not ask for help, though she now whispers the word, "Help," because she is so tired of longing, counting days, watching for the postman, letting her hand brush against the phone as a prayer for voice, words across time and space, "Hello? Hello?"

300 SOCIAL SCIENCES

The library is a small one, a suburban branch of the public system. It is a library for mothers and their children, for retirees. Sometimes there are students, scholars, like Sage Leary, who told her he was working on his Ph.D. in Spanish literature. Lorca and Cervantes.

"Why them?" she asked over dinner one evening, after he had stopped at the reference desk and asked Daphne to meet him.

"Spain," he said. "Have you ever seen Spain?"

"No," she said. "I've seen very few places outside Florida. Atlanta, Charleston, New York. Never Spain," she said. She sipped at her wine.

"Spain," he said. "Spain is a sunrise palette splashed across a midnight sky." He said Spain was black and dark—and yet, it was oranges and flowers, sidewalk cafes and cobblestone streets. It was slow and fast. Its rhythms changed as you moved through it. Spain, he said, was for the passionate. It was dance and wine, it was whistling men and old women carrying sacks of blood oranges. "It is beautiful," he said, raising his hands, offering his words. Beautiful.

She wanted to see Spain with Sage Leary.
He wanted to see it alone.

400 LANGUAGE

She remembers him practicing, whispering into her ear, his words wrapping, pulling, stretching her open. *Amor* and *beso*, he lightly traced her eyelashes, *ojos*, he'd say. Sometimes after wine and the right music, something bluesy and raw, he'd say *cuerpo* and *caliente,* his tongue like fire; he'd hold her hands, *manos*, and place them on himself and she would not question.

It was intoxicating, his words in her ears, but now she thinks that he will speak these phrases, endearments, into other faces. He will sing softly, *mi querida*, his mouth, *boca*, will linger and flutter against other collarbones.

500 NATURAL SCIENCES

One night he took her to an observatory, showed her constellations and told her stories, tracing the night sky along her neck and shoulders.

"Did you know that more than half of all the stars in our galaxy have one or more companion stars?" he said.

She did not know how to answer. "No," she finally said.

She wondered if it wasn't all too much, but she had waited for something like this, this vastness of sky and stars and stories for so long. Who was she to question science—chemistry, physics, the laws of attraction, the litmus tests of lust and love?

600 APPLIED SCIENCES

She preferred sandals. She wore Birkenstocks mostly, not because she was a hippie—she wasn't—

and not because she was an outdoors-type—which she was—but because they were comfortable, and she relied on comfort. "What is the point?" she asked about high heels, stilettos and slingbacks and shoes that sent the foot sliding and arcing into a C or an S.

"This is the point," her friend Nina had said, tapping with a manicured nail on the Guggenheim-carved heel of her black pump. "The curve of the calves, the swell of the hip with a good shoe. It's about anatomy."

"Anatomy," Daphne repeated.

"Try," Nina said.

Daphne went home with new shoes, and Sage Leary had made her lie down. He massaged her calves, her thighs, and said that indeed, it was about anatomy.

"This," he said, tracing a finger along her hamstring, "is a beautiful leg."

700 ARTS

Letters come in strange pattern, two in one day, none for a week, then one, then nothing, two weeks, then three, nothing.

And then.

A letter with photographs. The envelope is battered, as if he had stuffed it in a back pocket, left it sitting in Spain's sangria-dipped sun for weeks. The postmark is softened and blurred. Inside, a letter of travel, sights and sounds, and not very different from his own voice months ago: *It is oranges and flowers and sidewalk cafes and cobblestone streets.* There are postcard-like shots, buildings and doors and flowers, and one photo of

Sage: an outdoor café, a bottle of wine on a wrought-iron table, a smile, a slightly-tilted head, eyes hidden by sunglasses, and a leg, a slim leg and black shoe, a woman's lovely leg at the edge of the frame of the photo.

800 LITERATURE

He sends a poem. It is written in Spanish, Sage's spidery script, the flowery language indecipherable to Daphne. He does not send a translation. She stares at the words, pulls pieces of lines, *boca* and *beso* and *feliz*. At work, she looks for the Spanish/English dictionary he had used. It is not on the shelves and it pains her to think there is someone else reading his penciled margin notes, discovering what words are important to him.

900 GEOGRAPHY & HISTORY

She does not hear from him after the photos, the poem. She fears she has lost him to Spain. During her evening hours, she plans her trip, making notes on paper, travel guides spread across her table. She plans to track him in the castles of Toledo, the cathedrals of Salamanca, the hallways of Madrid's Prado. She presses pages to her face to smell the passion of Spain.

But at night, in her dreams, Sage stays always just ahead of her. He walks faster than Daphne can. He seems to know the doorways and side streets, the plazas and *palacios*, the places unnamed in her guide books. In her dreams, Sage Leary, one of those heavenly drifting boys, seems to be drifting further and further away, like translations of love poems tossed into a midnight wind.

Cyrus Is Spinning

Cyrus is spinning tonight the flyer on the thrift shop door says, so that when I push open the door, my palm touches my name and for a moment I feel like some kind of god. Then I think I'm just some beaten down god, the kind with wrinkled tunic and laurel wreath all askew, wine spills on my sandals. That's what I'm thinking, but that's not what others would think, not the crowds that come to the dance clubs to pump and shake and gyrate and almost fuck right there on the dance floor while I play the tunes. They chant "Cyrus!

Cyrus!" and they don't know how I hurt and hang my head at home, how I stare at my girlfriend's sleeping face and wonder just how to fix something that was once so good.

When I push open the Dusty Rose door, this little bell attached to a strand of Mardi Gras beads clangs against the glass, and there's this "hey" that comes from behind a big pile of clothes at the front counter. It's Sweet Marie. She's there every Saturday.

"You might like this," she says, holding up a blue guayabera. She's a pretty girl, with dark hair and pale white skin, and with that little black tank top she's wearing today, I take a long look at the tattoo that begins at the base of her throat and moves downward. A snake. Tongue flickering between her breasts.

I reach for the shirt. Stain-free. Soft.

"You okay?' she asks. "You look a bit beat."

I know. I look like hell. Not much sleep with me coming in at 4 a.m. and Jane waking up to tell me she's made a decision—she wants a baby. And then I said something about how she'd have to stop drinking her whiskey at noon and then there was this sort of passive fighting we do where we get real quiet and make sure our bodies don't touch in the bed, though it's only a full size mattress which means we're lying there real still.

"Not much sleep."

"Me neither," she says, and I think it's because she's having lots of sex, sweat beading on that snakeskin, her skinny little body all angles and movement.

I smile. She smiles. The phone rings. She picks it up and the way she says, "Hey there," I know she's talking to her boyfriend. That's the way Jane used to speak to me, until she got all blue and angry.

I head over to the pants section and breathe deeply. There's a lot I like about thrift shops. I like the smell of sandalwood and cigarettes and laundry detergent. This one in particular has this other smell, which is Sweet Marie, something flowery, one of those smells for soothing the soul.

I like the idea of taking on a bit of someone else's vibe. That's what's cool about thrift shops.

"You ever try fortune telling?" Sweet Marie calls out to me.

I turn to her. "Nah. Why?"

"Coffee grounds," she says. "Just found this book that helps you figure it," and she holds up a paperback.

"What's your cup telling you?"

"Well," she says, but then the phone rings again. Her voice gets all hushed and low. I grab a pair of jeans and a pair of wool trousers.

I skim the coats section and pick out a nice green corduroy blazer. Maybe some English professor wore it with a pair of jeans and black cowboy boots. The girls in the class would think he was great, maybe a bit too old, but great. The guys would hate him at first, but then they'd see he was a good guy. They'd want to drink beers with him, but he'd say things like, "Got to get home to the wife."

I could be into that—looking like a professor. Especially when I put my glasses on. Jane says I look wicked smart then and she wants to have sex, which is good by me. Except Jane left the house this morning without a note, after we spent the night like two corpses there in the bed, nobody turning or shifting.

"Hey," I shout over to Marie. She still has the phone to her ear, her lips pursed together. I motion that I'm heading to a dressing room.

"I'm not happy here," Jane says to me the other day. "It's not the right market for me." She's an artist, makes fancy marble sculptures. She says she needs to get out of this college town and go to a bigger city. "More cultured," she says.

"But I'm happy here," I tell her. I'm an east coaster, a southern boy, I say, because she's talking about California.

Maybe Jane's headed out west, I think as I look in the mirror. Got herself in the car, dancing in her seat to the bad radio tunes she likes.

"Cyrus." I hear Sweet Marie's voice outside my dressing room.

"Yeah?"

"Decent?"

I've got the pair of jeans on. My own tee-shirt. "Yeah."

Marie slides the curtain open, peers in.

"I like the music you play at the clubs. You're good at reading the crowd." She smiles. Her lips are now painted this pale pink, frosty like window glass in winter.

"Thanks."

"Mind if I come in?" And I guess it doesn't matter if I mind, because she's squeezed herself into the dressing room, her face lifted upward. She is tiny.

Her tongue pushes out, rests on her top lip. The snake moves as she breathes.

I'm thinking, oh man, oh man, but then I lean down and kiss her, and hell if I know why, maybe it's the guy whose jeans these were, maybe he was one of those guys who gets love in a dressing room, but something's going on and I'm kissing Sweet Marie.

"You smell nice," I say.

"Jasmine."

And that's when the bell on the door clangs and a man's voice, "Marie," booms into the shop.

"*Merde*," she whispers, and I'm thinking, "Oh God, she's French," and it's these jeans I just know it, but my lips linger, my hand squeezes her hip one moment longer. She runs her hand over her denim miniskirt. She sticks out her lower lip like a little girl pouting, and then she moves the dressing room curtain slightly, letting herself out into the store.

"Gerald," she calls out, and I tug at the vinyl curtain of pink and green stripes, making sure it's all the way closed. One of the rings sticks on the pole, ripping the curtain. It makes a popping sound.

The music in the store is turned louder. Afro-Caribbean. Good dance beat.

I put my own pants back on quickly. I stare in the mirror, wiping at the pink frost smeared on my lips. *Merde*. I pull open the curtain.

Nobody. There's nobody in the store and it's a tiny place, nowhere to hide. I walk up to the front counter. Sweet Marie's fortune telling book is there. So is her cup of coffee. I peek. It's half full, so I can't tell what's gonna happen. But I want the blazer, the guayabera, and the jeans. And on top of that pile of clothes Marie's been working through is this pair of shoes, brown leather Rockports. Size ten.

"Nice." I pick them up. The soles are only slightly worn so I slip them on. Heels, toes, all balanced. I check my wallet, lay $20 on the counter right next to the coffee cup. I swear I consider drinking that coffee so I can see what I find, but I don't. I throw the clothes I want over my shoulder and I'm out.

The afternoon light is startling. Marie and Gerald are leaning up against the storefront wall. Gerald's got a cigarette dangling from his lips. He's large, wide like a truck. Marie waves. I smile, turn the other way, and as I'm moving, trying to take it all slow, I hear Sweet Marie call, "Thanks. Come again." I nod and continue down the sidewalk, old shoes in hand.

Petals

In the late afternoon sun wash, the wrangle and roar of traffic reaches a feverish hum so that Miami's air is thick with heat and insult, men in their cars loosening their ties, women peeling down pantyhose and cracking cramped toes, kids in the backseats shouting songs, truckers popping tallboys in paper bags, and strit-strutting among the stopped cars, smiles pasted to their faces, are Lydia and Yvonne, the flower sellers of US1 and Ludlum. In their short shorts and cheap sandals, their tank tops and push-up bras, the ladies smile and parade the spaces between cars, holding bundles of carnations, pinks, whites, an occasional yellow, frail petals limping in their hands. They try to meet heavy-lidded eyes, to sell a bouquet or two. They watch the light, red to green, and they hurry back to the sidewalk and drop their bundles in buckets, sigh, wait for the next light change.

Across the street, a man sells doughnuts. He carries boxes stacked atop each other, a dozen glazed doughnuts to take home for dessert, for tomorrow's breakfast, to eat on the long drive home. At the green light, he sits down in a canvas chair he has placed on the sidewalk. He leans back and tilts his chin to the sky.

"He is beautiful, no?" Lydia asks Yvonne. Lydia is in love with the doughnut man who is there across the intersection on Tuesdays and Fridays. He is too young for her. She is full and heavy from hard living and this man is just a boy not too long ago done with high school, but still he is handsome, and Lydia at thirty is lonely and Lydia can dream.

But Yvonne will not let her. Yvonne who is younger, twenty-two, says, "*Muy guapo.*"

Yvonne is pregnant and has yet to tell her boyfriend Paul, for surely he will shout and maybe hit her, drive off in his car and never return. She pauses, squinting through sunglasses that shield tired-red eyes, and then she continues, "Better for me. Too beautiful for you," and the way she says it is mean and ugly and Lydia turns to look at her cousin with surprise.

"Too beautiful for me?" Lydia says. She holds her drink away from her lips and notes the half-chewed straw before she stares at Yvonne's face.

Yvonne knows she has said a mean thing, but still, it is a truth, Lydia is too old and not very attractive.

So Yvonne just says, "*Lo siento.* I'm tired. I'm hot. I'm sorry."

But Lydia will not have it. No, no, no, she puts her drink down on the sidewalk; she straightens and shoves her hands on her big hips. "He wouldn't want you either," Lydia says. "Pregnant little whore." The words come out before she has really thought about them, as if the heat of the day forced her words, they exhale, collide with car horns and blasts of loud music. They slap Yvonne across the face.

Perhaps it is true. Yvonne has not told Paul about her pregnancy because it might not be his baby. It could be George's baby. Maybe. But how dare Lydia. And how, Yvonne wonders, does Lydia even know about the baby? She has not said a word, not a thing to her cousin. "At least," Yvonne says, "at least, a man will sleep with me."

The light changes and the women stay where they are on the sidewalk, the cars pulling to a stop, the drivers sighing and swearing, and Lydia and Yvonne glare, they force furrowed brows and wrinkle-tightened mouths, and finally the two women reach down into the water buckets and pick up their bundles of flowers. Across the intersection, the handsome one weaves in and out of lanes. He is smiling, his teeth so white against his tanned skin, his jeans low on his slim waist. He glances at the flower ladies and maybe he smiles at them.

"Whore," Lydia says again, and she smiles her widest smile toward the handsome one.

"Virgin," Yvonne says, and then smack, she slaps Lydia across the face with her bundle of carnations.

Oh.

Lydia swings back and there are flowers, flowers in flight, petals soaring and sailing and the air thick with color and scent and the women flailing, retreating and attacking, tattered stems like whips across their arms and cheeks, the ground littered with floral confetti. And then Yvonne feels herself weaken, her knees buckle, the world pinpoints from blue to white to black. She wishes for the handsome man to rescue her, and she falls.

"No, no, no," Lydia says, and she drops her stems and falls to her knees and puts her hand to Yvonne's forehead. "*Dios, Dios, Dios,*" she chants, and while she is invoking prayer, while she is thinking she is the worst woman in the world, the ugliest, meanest woman in the world, she looks up and dodging cars with doughnut boxes in his hands is the handsome one. He rushes toward them, and for just the briefest moment, Lydia thinks that he is coming for her. She begins to cry, and her hands sweep the ground, gathering up petals.

Round

After we spend an hour arguing about who said what, we catch the last hour of the televised State Spelling Bee. We're on the couch and Jed is smoking a joint he found tucked in his shirt pocket. He shuts his eyes, leans back and blows a stream of smoke upward as Rupert McIntosh asks for the definition of NYCTALOPIA.

"A condition of the eyes in which sight is abnormally poor or wholly gone at night or in dim light," the moderator says.

Rupert spells it NYCT-O-LOPIA.

"Otherwise known as night blindness," Jed says, his eyes still closed.

I take the joint from Jed and suck deep. Rupert sits down next to his mother. She grabs the frail boy into her big arms. She looks like the greeter at our Walmart who always says, "Have a bless-ed day."

I cough and cough again, place the joint in the ashtray on the table in front of me. The ashtray is one I made in elementary school ceramics, a lopsided shallow bowl that my mother re-gifted me.

"I have nyctalopia," I say. I rub my eyes hard enough that my left contact lens moves in my eye. I blink several times and try to push it with my finger.

"You have narcolepsy, Nora," he says.

"Funny," I say. "Necrophiliac."

"Necco Wafers," he says.

"Pink," I say.

"Black."

"Diaphanous," Olive says on television.

Olive Silverman is the only girl left in the Bee. She sits there with the boys, her blonde hair in two pigtails, low ones, messy skatergirl hip. She doesn't look like a Beehead."Diaphanous," Olive says again. She blinks her eyes slowly then closes them.

"Narcolepsy," Jed says.

"D-I-A-P-H-A-N-O-U-S," Olive says.

She's so smart. According to the mini-vignettes they show about the participants, Olive likes chess and knitting. She also plays guitar. She wants to be an environmental lawyer. She's twelve, and I'm pretty sure boys love her. I think all the boys at the Bee must have hoped for the seat next to Olive.

"Correct," Bee Man says and Olives smiles, tugs at one of her pigtails and returns to her seat. David Li gives her a high five. He's a good sport because Olive Silverman is going to take him down. I can feel it. I want to say, David, don't even try. She'll break your heart.

"I could have been Olive," I say.

"We could learn a new word a day," Jed says. "Get one of those calendars."

"We could." I take the joint back from Jed, who has rescued it from the ashtray. But I know we won't. It's like this sometimes, our desire to improve ourselves. A few months ago it was our new-recipe-a-week idea. This lasted two weeks. Jed cooked Rosemary-Lemon Potatoes and I made Linguini with White Bean Sauce and then the cookbooks were buried in the wicker basket with novels, sneakers, and the *New Yorkers* that come too often.

"Verisimilitude," the announcer says. Rohit Patel stands rigid. His arms are at his sides. His eyes widen as if he is shocked.

"Language of origin," he says.

"Latin."

Rohit nods. His body is almost motionless. "Verisimilitude."

Rohit spells it wrong. He adds an 'e' in the middle. His eyes widen. He cracks his knuckles.

"Poor Rohit," I say when he shuffles over to his father and mother. His mother wipes at his cheek. His father pats his shoulder. Rohit plays tennis and writes fantasy stories and idolizes J.R.R. Tolkien.

At a commercial break I tell Jed how I was a spelling bee loser. Fifth grade, Maplewood Elementary, out on the word TRULY.

"I put the 'e' in it," I say. I stand to stretch. Our sofa is too soft. I kink my neck in the evenings. "Truly. I knew I was wrong. I had a choice—e or no e. I'm so bad at choices," I say.

"Well," Jed says because he knows it is true.

"My teacher, Mrs. Hurley, said to me, 'I expected you would win, Nora.'"

"Mrs. Hurley made you feel bad."

"I didn't like her," I say. "She smelled like dog food."

David Li is about to get his word. David wants to design computer games for a living. He has already created a game called "Rubble." It has something to do with wrecking things. I don't see David as destructive; I see him as twelve. I know twelve. I teach middle school art. David's word is LEGERDEMAIN. I cheer for him. Since Rohit is out, I want David to join Olive in the finals. But then he will lose, because Olive will bat her blue eyes and David will melt. He will be reduced to rubble.

David spells his word correctly. He does it and smiles before the announcer can even say he is correct. David is confident.

"Truly!" I shout. "T-R-U-L-Y!"

"You do that too much," Jed says.

"What?"

"You look at what you did wrong, not right."

I stare at the television. Donny Bell is the last speller for the round. He looks pained. I worry he's going to throw up on television.

"Look at me," I say. "Look at them," I say, waving a hand at Donny Bell and his bright red hair.

"What about them?"

"Fucking brilliant." I head to the kitchen to refill my wine glass. "I could have been brilliant," I shout to Jed. "Somewhere I went wrong."

Wrong includes too much wine, probably. And Jed, possibly. My ex-husband, whom I actually like, thinks Jed is no good. "He has no ambition," Saul says. "He's a slacker," my mother says. I hate it when she uses words she's never used before.

He's kind, I want to say. But everyone scoffs at that. Like kindness is easy.

Right now Jed works in a dive shop. He's a guitarist, really, and he works odd jobs because he's not making much with his band. He's brilliant though, on guitar, and that's why I fell in love with him. I have a thing for brilliance, even though sometimes, as I found out with my ex-husband, brilliance means distance, vagary, a sense of being and not being.

"Donny's still in," Jed says when I return to the couch with a full glass of wine. "You know, these kids are just kids."

"Really smart kids."

"True. But who's to say that Olive Silverman isn't going to get drunk and sleep with some guy and get pregnant and go live in Idaho."

"No."

"Yes. And she'll write marketing campaigns for potatoes until she realizes she's had it. Then she'll go on Prozac and leave her husband and go live on South Beach and walk around grocery stores in a bikini."

"Don't blaspheme Olive," I say.

Jed sighs. "Want me to turn this off?"

"No!" I sip my wine, watch my spellers. David Li goes out on FORMALDEHYDE.

Which leaves Olive and Donny.

How to say to Jed, without bruising his sweet heart, that I'm worried. Here we are, midway through our thirties, and it doesn't seem like there is much else. This is it. Not brilliant.

I just say it. The wine has made me melancholy, not silly.

"Because we're not in the Spelling Bee?" he asks.

"Yes," I say, even though it doesn't make sense.

"I'll go buy that word-a-day calendar tomorrow," he says.

I smile and shake my head. Expectations are high. Failure is near. Sometimes it is all I can taste.

Olive wins the Bee. She spells BACCALAUREATE. I cheer, clap, slug the rest of my wine, while Olive tugs at her pigtails. Her parents and younger sister circle her in a group hug.

"Come," Jed says. "Let's F-O-R-N-I-C-A-T-E." He leads me to the bedroom.

Later, before we fall asleep, I am curled into Jed's body, spooned, and his right hand cups my breast.

"What is the entomology of fornicate?" I ask.

"You mean etymology. Entomology is the study of insects."

"Etymology," I say. Sometimes Jed surprises me and this keeps me going.

"Sweet dreams," he says. "Truly."

E or no e. There is nothing truly wrong here. Truly nothing wrong. I keep repeating the words, flipping them around, waiting for the letters to fall into place.

Nothing wrong, truly. Jed's snores buzz through the darkness, which is not real darkness. The moon is full enough that I can see light through the window blinds. For a moment, I consider pulling away and edging closer to my side of the bed. But I don't.

Lane 12

Dare to dream, tattooed bowling queen, with your lemon yellow fleecy flounced t-shirt, sleeves cut to show your muscled arms, your lime green satin pants tight like whiskey down a throat, your red ringlet curls pulled high in a ponytail fountain. Take off your sunglasses, pop another piece of gum, it's time, sweet Juney Teresa Hart, to take the kingpin, take the hooks and wicked wrist twists, it's time to bring it on home for the Marion Four.

Catcalls and hootie hollers and finger snaps and leg slaps, as Juney Teresa Hart, the tattooed bowling queen of Majestic Lanes, makes her way to lane 12 for some cosmic karaoke bowling. Tuesday nights—cheap beer and cheese fries for two bucks. Rudy the Rude Dog Manager plugging in equipment, tap tapping on the microphone, slapping shoes on the counter, *line 'em up, sixes and nines and no more elevens, nope, got to wear twelves*, but not for JTH, Miss Juney Teresa Hart, she's got her own shoes, custom designed—sweet toeless slingbacks with red glitter stripes. She's got her shoe size, *7*, tattooed on the backs of her ankles, she's got *Bowl or Die* tattooed just above her left breast, she's got her gold-flecked ball, initials carved in black, in a green velvet bag. She's ready.

Ooowee, Bowling Queen, she hears and she smiles, she tilts her head, she licks her lower lip and laughs, a laugh like wind chimes dipped in peanut butter pie. She gives a thumbs up with her bowling thumb, rubbed and primed with sweet almond cream. She puckers her pink painted lips and blows kisses to her teammates at the bar, Wilbur and Crazy Paula and Captain Hook, she struts on by Rudy the Rude Dog, who stops slapping shoes, and she pauses at lane 12, breathes in, her lemon yellow fleecy flounced t-shirt tight across her tattooed chest, and exhales a lingering puff of peppermint.

Crazy Paula joins her, hands Juney a beer, and says, "How you feeling, Juney Teresa Hart?" And just for a moment, Juney pauses, a moment so brief nobody would notice it—not even Shy Wilbur, who loves Juney Teresa Hart, who here at the bowling alley can't get past his blushing hellos though at home he has brilliant conversations with her picture, a photo clipped from the newspaper and hung on his refrigerator; he talks to sweet Juney while he makes his eggs in the morning, while he drinks his Bushmills at night.

Juney pauses, then she smiles and says, "I'm doing okay, Paula, I'm doing okay." She lets her chewing gum snap, and Juney Teresa Hart puts her green velvet bag down, takes a swig of beer and says, "Let's bowl."

Only Crazy Paula knows that Juney Teresa Hart is filled to the brim with sorrow, that the man she called her Demon Lover, the man she called Wish Come True, had taken her tattooed heart and torn it asunder just last month when he said, "Juney Teresa Hart, I think I've got to go back to Analee." "Going back?" Juney Teresa Hart had said. "Going back? But why?" She just couldn't believe it, the world had surely gone crazy, the cosmos had surely gone from Technicolor to gray, just how, why, oh why, why, why was Mister Decker Pancake going back to Analee? How ridiculous, Analee Pancake, who couldn't even bowl a 120, not even on Bumpers Up Night, not even with the full moon shining like a pearly bowling ball in the sky. Going back to Analee?

But Juney Teresa Hart is trying to get over it, she's cried her tears, she's tossed shoes at walls like she's throwing strikes, she's cursed the name of Decker Pancake, she's dreamed of his bowling ball cracking and splintering like splits, and so tonight, with the lights dimming and the disco ball spinning diamond flecks, and the sound of pins crashing, the sound of balls thumping on slicked floorboards, she says, "I'm doing okay."

Juney Teresa Hart is trying hard to be classy, so she doesn't send an evil eye toward lane 9, and she doesn't spit when Rudy calls out over the intercom that Decker has a call at the front desk, she just sits down at lane 12 and types in her name for the scoreboard, JUNE BUG, and she punches the letters with sure-fingered swiftness.

Shy Wilbur slides into the seat next to Juney, he gives her a quick smile, he says, "Looking good, Juney," and he says it like a crackled whisper. "Why thank you, Wilbur," she says and she smiles, he smiles, she notices how white his teeth are, quite nice actually, much nicer than Decker's coffee-stained yellows.

"Cosmic!" The word comes like a psychotic dream voice, it blares along lanes and reverberates in the gutters and it repeats, "Awwwwww, yeah, cosmic," and the words through the intercom signify the start of cosmic karaoke night, stroke of eleven, the neon tubing starts to blink and shiver, then full force pink and green and orange lines of color brighten the walls and pin holders.

Cheers go upward, yahoos and yeehaws and yippeedees, and fists pump air and hands slap knees and backsides. Beers are slugged and shoes are laced and stomped, except Juney Teresa Hart whose shoes don't tie, and Juney pulls her gold ball from her bag and sets it next to Shy Wilbur's blue-grey duotone, and once again, "Cosmic! Oh yeah, it's cosmic," bounces through the intercom system and a siren wail, a bullhorn call, and Juney checks that the straps of her slingbacks aren't covering her number sevens, and then she looks to the front desk where Rudy with his pompadour wig and his Buddy Holly glasses is grinning wide, the microphone to his mouth, and a quick glance toward lane 9, and damn it all to hell, Juney's eyes meet Decker's, he's staring right at her, his mouth moves and she turns, spins in her glittery shoes before she can see what he's saying.

Damn it all to hell, Decker Pancake, with your shiny black hair and your wicked-ass grin and your hands that can palm a bowling ball and the curve of a woman's hip with the same ease. And damn you too, Analee Pancake, with your simpering whine about wifehood and your begging and your knowledge that a man like Decker Pancake likes to be begged.

"You're up," Captain Hook calls out, and Juney grabs her ball, fits her soft fingers into the holes, pauses, steps, steps, lets the ball go, she sees pins explode, she sees the lights flash, she sees the neon bulbs brighten, she hears "Cosmic, get your cosmic on," and she turns, a strike, and there's Decker on his lane, his tongue stuck out in concentration, and she hurries back before she has to watch, Decker, Decker, everywhere.

A voice like a turkey shot and dying now rises above the din of pins falling and balls tumbling, and Turbo Terry is at the karaoke machine singing "Rock Lobster" and things seem just a bit too tweaked, a bit too much for the bowling queen, she's got to sit down, have a drink, she feels her sorrow like one pin standing, she feels herself tensing, tightening, she feels like maybe, just maybe, she's not going to make it through the night.

"You okay?' she hears, and she opens her eyes and Shy Wilbur is crouched before her, and she says, "I'm okay," because that's what JTH is all about, being okay, even if Decker Pancake is just three lanes away and looking at her again.

"You're up," Crazy Paula calls out, and this is how it seems to go, with bowlers up and down and frame two, three, four, five, Juney noticing that a blister might be forming on one foot, and this has never happened with her customized bowling shoes, but tonight, yes, a little rubbing, a little irritation, and Freddy at the karaoke machine singing "Heartbreak Hotel" during frame six and folks booing Freddy because Freddy has a voice like an old monkey crying, and there's Juney Teresa Hart with a not-so-impressive 106 in the seventh frame.

"Cosmic, dynamite, out of sight, it's cosmic night," Rudy with the microphone, his grin grown wider, and eight, nine, ten, tenth frame wind-up, with Juney Teresa Hart softly tracing the outline of her *Bowl or Die* tattoo, refusing to turn at the sound of Decker's calls, "June Bug, June Bug, please, please, please."

"You're up," Paula says, and Juney stands. She limps just a bit with the blister maybe getting bigger, and she takes her ball, bought on her thirty-fifth birthday, and she stands before lane 12, and she's about to take her first step when the karaoke machine starts up again and she hears "This one's for you, June Bug," and there's Decker singing and his voice is of course not like a turkey or a monkey at all, but more like fire, and she doesn't know why it happens or how it happens but that ball slips out of her hand and downward and those toeless slingbacks don't do much for a girl sometimes, and she howls and curses and falls like a fluttering leaf, like a silk slip dropping. She sits down on the lane, and Decker Pancake with his redemption song stops mid-line while he stares at Juney Teresa Hart.

"It's cos..." Rudy begins, but he too sees Juney the tattooed bowling queen sitting down on lane 12, and he stops, he says into the microphone, "Juney?" and she grits her teeth and stares at her toes and shakes her head and listens to the silence around her. Freeze frame, with bowlers paused eating cheese fries and pizza slices, and bowlers powdering fingers and bowlers talking stocks and bonds and bowlers clapping for a nailed spare and bowlers dancing to the line, and everyone pauses to look to lane 12.

"You okay?" she hears in her ear, and crouched before her again is Shy Wilbur, and he's got his arm on her shoulder and his eyes are specked with the same gold as her bowling ball. "You okay?" he asks, and Juney says, "I don't think so," and she lets Wilbur help her up, she smiles as he lifts her in his shy arms and carries her away from lane 12 while the neon lights flash and the disco ball spins, and Juney Teresa Hart lets Shy Wilbur dare to dream.

The End of *Stick Man and Hat Head:* The Comic Drawn Almost Daily During Mr. Ryan's Sixth Grade Science Class, Period 4

Stick Man is really cool even though he's sort of quiet and only a stick figure. (*Ha ha to Mrs. Garcia the art teacher who says, "Sam, stick figures need clothes."*) Usually Stick Man's arms are down. Sometimes he is trying to make a point, and then his stick arms stick (*Ha!*) straight out to the sides, or straight up in the air in a V like he is a cheerleader. (*Mindi, who sits in front of Sam, is a cheerleader. She's nice! She plays piano!*)

Hat Head is Stick Man's arch enemy. Hat Head is not cool. He's a jerk (*just like Henry in the second row*).

He looks very much like Stick Man, except Hat Head wears a hat, which is actually a rectangle topped by a small square. Usually the comic is about Stick Man and Hat Head fighting with swords or doing somersaults and backflips like ninjas or doing karate chops that mean karate chops because one stick arm is up and one is down and there's a messy "Ha-yah!!!" with three exclamation points in a word balloon. (*"Neatness counts," Mrs. Denny always says with a sigh during essay time.)* Sometimes Stick Man and Hat Head fence with foils too, and then they shout things like "Touché!" and "Epee!" and other terms learned at the Elite Fencing Academy on Archer Road on Thursday afternoons.

One day (*while Mr. Ryan talks about igneous rocks*) Stick Man is in another fencing duel with Hat Head when Mindi turns around and smiles. When she turns back, Stick Man knocks Hat Head's hat to the ground with his foil. Without his hat, Hat Head's head falls off. It rolls and tumbles. (*The idea for a flip book is born.*) Stick Man says, "Ha! Ha! Ha!" and Hat Head's head says, "Argh," and Hat Head's head closes its eyes into X's and sticks out its oval tongue. Stick Man knows Hat Head will try to return with his head glued back on because Hat Head always returns for more ass-kicking. But Stick Man is ready. When Hat Head creeps back, stick arms struggling to hold his head on, Stick Man gives him a WHACK! CLONK! And with one big kick to the stick solar plexus, THUMP, Hat Head's head and body fly off the page. Out of the picture. "That's the real end of you," Stick Man says. Mindi turns around and asks for a pencil. Stick Man raises his arms in a V for victory.

Parade of Champions

Behold, behold, coming across the front lawn, the Parade of Champions, whistles please, kazoos and trumpets and triangles ting-tinging, gather ye confetti while ye may, toss, laugh, toss, here they come, giggle and circumstance and clap, clap, louder everyone, louder, it is them, in all their splendor, the Zeller Sisters, Street Tennis Champions of America. See the one with a colander on her head, carrying her racket like a guitar, that's the older sister, she's eight, and the other one, with a catcher's mask atop her head, wearing sunglasses and carrying her tennis racket upright like a torch, she's seven. The younger one hums so her lips tingle, her throat tickles, she hums a song she's learned in school, "Oklahoma!", and the song has nothing to do with the Parade of Champions, but she likes it, waving wheat smelling sweet. The older sister air-guitars with her racket, and her song, which she sings in her head, is a song she really doesn't know, it's an amalgam of sound, it's loud and similar to the music she hears coming from the next-door-neighbor boy's bedroom window. The two sisters spy on him sometimes, they peer in his window and watch the boy on his computer, the boy on the phone, the boy lifting weights, the boy kissing his girlfriend, and today, at the Parade of Champions, hoorah, hoorah, the older sister sings one of his songs because maybe she has a crush on him, even though he's older by years and years. The two sisters march across the lawn, back and forth, back and forth, getting ready to play the final match in their ten game tournament, which started last Sunday when they found two tennis rackets in the hallway closet, along with an old Ouija board and a ripped up vinyl Twister mat, and yes, it becomes their sport, street tennis with costuming, black cowboy hat, gauzy scarf, red cape, mismatched socks. Today, for the championship, a colander, a catcher's mask, and names, names created just for today, names created over breakfast, the power breakfast of champions, chocolate milk and cinnamon rolls and slices of salami. Queen You Can't See My Serve It's So Fast is the younger sister, she picks her name first and then the older sister, not to be outdone, announces she will be Supersonic Speedster of Mythic Proportions, the Mythic Proportions part being an addendum, something she has heard her teacher say, so that when it is time for her to proclaim her championship name, she says, "And I am Supersonic Speedster," and she sees her sister roll her eyes, and she pauses, adds, "Of Mythic Proportions" and her sister's eyes stop rolling. After breakfast, after their grand namings, the girls put on their game-day costumes and head out the door to the lawn where they parade, they high-step, waving at the crowd, and then they stand, rackets by their sides, they hear the hoots and claps, they hear "Go Queen! Go Queen!" and "Win this one, Supersonic!" The girls smile, they shake hands, and what they don't know is that the neighbor boy is at his window watching, and he is smiling, remembering when he and his brother used to play Greatest Catches in the Universe, and his girlfriend, who is standing next to him, is smiling, because she's remembering Fabulous Circus, the girlfriend and her two best friends doing somersaults and handstands, throwing tasselled batons high in the air and spinning, spinning and stopping just in time to catch the falling batons, and she too can hear the wild cheering, the applause, it goes on and on until the Zeller Sisters step onto the street court, and then all is silly quiet so the game may begin.

Shellie Zacharia's stories have appeared in *Hobart, Opium, Keyhole Magazine, Canteen, The Pinch, Washington Square, Beloit Fiction,* and elsewhere. She lives in Gainesville, Florida.